SUN, SEA, THE BILLIONAIRE AND ME

A Romantic Comedy

HARMONY KNIGHT

Chapter 1

I'd like to go on record as disagreeing with Ben Franklin. He was dead wrong about the certainties of life; there are in fact *three* things that are certain, not two. Death—obviously. Taxes—to a varying degree, though I imagine the tax bill of the average barista is a more significant pain in the ass than that of the average billionaire. And the third certainty of life is that any time things seem to be going well for me, Franchesca Jane Potts, of Meadow Hill, Upstate New York, the universe will throw me a curve ball to knock me back on my ass.

A mere moment ago, I was standing on a stunningly adorned pier over a shimmering lake, wearing the most expensive garment that's ever touched my freckled skin, grinning like a fool as my best friend, Robbie, said "I do" and kissed Matt, the handsome billionaire she's marrying today. Everything was perfection. I felt like a princess holding my maid of honor bouquet, and Robbie looked like a queen in her stunning ivory bridal gown. Tiny white rabbits hopped about on the grass in front of the vast mansion in the middle of the estate, Egyptian geese waddled back and forth serenely around the wedding party, and the lake was alive with all manner of beautiful fish—a result of the native Floridian alligators being unable to get through the perimeter fence, according to the greeter who gave me a tour when I arrived a few days ago.

And now? Now, I'm standing in a freezing lake full of disgusting slimy fish, dripping and breathless. I guess the cheer that went up as the pastor announced that "you may kiss the bride" must've startled the geese, because one of them started honking like a hyperactive trucker, apparently decided that I was to blame for the commotion, fixed me in its sights, and charged straight at me. I barely even saw it coming, it was just a blur of flapping and honking. Understandably startled at the sight of this feathery missile screaming towards me, I jumped backward, felt my foot catch on the hem of my gown, and heard a gasp go up among the rest of the wedding party as I fell ass-over-tits backward. And halfway through my fall, I realized, as thoughts came to me as fast as light and time slowed to a syrupy drip, that the only thing behind me was a large expanse of glassy water. The cold rush that swept over me as I crashed through the surface snapped me back to reality, and I gasped as I tried to keep my head above the water.

"I... the goose... it came straight for me!" I cry as I struggle to stand back up in the chest-high water, plucking a string of pond weed from my beautifully embroidered bust, and then immediately close my mouth to try and stop myself from swallowing any gross lake water. Even as the water runs down over my face and drips from free tendrils of what had been a beautiful up-do, I can feel a hot flush creeping up my chest and neck. And then I hear a deep voice coming from the pier, echoing across the lake.

"Don't worry, I've got you."

I turn to see Jonah, Matt's business partner and the best man at this wedding, jumping down into the lake beside me.

This is all I need. The super-hot, billionaire best man—with whom I have been flirting outrageously every single time we've been in the same room (though to be fair, he's been giving as good as he got)—pulling my soggy, sodden ass out of the lake.

"Oh, my God," I say quietly. "This is mortifying."

Jonah scoops me up with a grunt—I guess my waterlogged dress *is* pretty heavy—and heads for shore with me in his arms. Instinctively, I grab around his neck.

"It's not *that* mortifying," he says, with a slight smirk. "Besides, you brought a bit of excitement to the ceremony. Weddings are always so dull."

"It's still mortifying," I say, stubbornly. I can hear a loud guffaw of laughter coming from the wedding party, and I know immediately that it's Robbie's sister, Anna. Of course, she finds the whole thing hilarious, and she doesn't have nearly enough decorum to disguise it. I groan to myself as I realize that I'm gonna be hearing about this forever.

"We require a change of clothes," says Jonah theatrically, addressing the whole gathering. His deep voice is loud and clear. "Farewell for now."

I guess he's used to speaking in board rooms and being the boss, so it shouldn't surprise me as much as it does when he addresses the entire, snickering congregation with such confidence—and it definitely shouldn't make my stomach flip the way it does.

"God," I huff under my breath, burying my bright red face in Jonah's chest as Anna's laughter keeps coming in gales, chasing us up the lawn. "She's so immature."

He seems a little tense. Stony-faced, and with his arms almost rigid under my legs and across my back. Then again, he is carrying one hundred and fifty-ish pounds of woman and probably not far off that weight of water and woven silk.

"Where's your room?" he asks when we get into the mansion house.

Finally lifting my head now that it seems I won't have to suffer the indignity of everyone's laughter, I groan. "Robbie's mom has my key in her purse," I say.

Technically, he could put me down now and let me drip dry on the marble floor like a wayward umbrella. But he keeps hold of me, the warmth of his arms and his chest seeping through the fabric and the pond weed and the wet, and neither of us mentions it.

Jonah looks at me, his ocean blue eyes closer than they've ever been before, and I feel momentarily like my heart has stopped. Which would be just my luck, really, but only about two in one hundred thousand people my age will have a heart attack each year, so I'm probably safe.

This is why I like numbers. They're certain. Comforting.

"Right," says Jonah, nodding his head once, decisively, which causes a lock of his sandy blond hair to fall down onto his forehead. My fingers itch to reach up and push it back into place, but I resist.

"You can shower in my room, and I'll send someone to get you a change of clothes," he says and starts walking.

4

There's a part of me that wants to protest the confident ease with which he just *decides* what will happen with the air of a man whose words are magical incantations that set the world in motion. But since that would likely result in me having to squelch my way back down to the lakeside to fetch my keys from Brenda's clutch, I keep my mouth shut.

"I'll call Anna if you let me use your phone," I say, feeling a need to fill the silent gaps between his steps. "I'm sharing with her anyway, so she can fetch my evening dress from our room."

"Sure," says Jonah, approaching the door of his suite.

He places me down gently on the floor and holds my upper arms as I wobble a little under the weight of the dress. Who knew water could be so heavy?

"I wonder how many gallons of water are in this thing," I say, looking down at my gown to avoid looking up at the man. Flirting in the company of friends is a very different thing from flirting in the privacy of a deserted mansion hallway—especially when you're about to go into someone's bedroom. It would all feel very Jane Austen if I weren't so… wet. Ahem.

Jonah pulls his wallet out of his pocket, turns it upside down, and lets some water drip to the floor, then grabs his key card and presses it against the lock. A quiet beep later, he opens the door and stands back, motioning me to go inside.

That's when I notice how completely ruined his suit is. There are streaks of brown and green all over it. Pondweed here, feathers there. With a sudden flush of panic, I walk quickly inside.

"Is there a mirror?" I ask.

Jonah saunters in and throws his wallet down on a side table, closing the door behind him. He looks over at me, his eyes trailing from hem to head and back again. My throat constricts at the way he looks at me, my tummy flips, my breath hitches in my throat—and then I realize that I have completely imagined any spark of attraction I might have read in his eyes. He's looking at me because I'm a waterlogged mess.

"Over there," he says as he pulls his jacket off. He nods to a door that leads off the sitting room.

And of *course* there's a sitting room. Not that the room I'm sharing with Anna isn't beautiful—the whole mansion is stunning—but it's a beautiful double room with a nice seating area near the window. Jonah's room is almost as big and fancy as the bridal suite.

I head for the door, into the bedroom, and straight across to the full-length mirror on the far side. It's way, way worse than I thought. The entire bottom half of the dress is just a gross mess of pond weed, brown and green smears, and little bits of something caught in the gaps between the intricately embroidered flowers on the long skirt.

"It's ruined," I whisper, feeling a lump forming in my throat. My voice crackles with emotion as I stare at the destruction.

"So what?" asks Jonah, nonchalant. I didn't even hear him come into the room behind me. "The wedding's over."

"That's not the point," I say, looking up at his reflection in the mirror. He's across the room, beside the bed, and what-ever I was about to say is completely lost when I see that he's already stripped out of his sodden suit and is standing there in nothing but black boxer briefs.

6

I'm not usually the type to be caught short by a good-looking man. I'm not unattractive and I have a Tinder account, so I've seen my fair share of men in all sorts of states of undress, whether I wanted to or not. But this man is something else.

He's not movie-star huge and he doesn't look like he's just spent a month chugging raw eggs and broccoli to define his abs, but he is broad and muscular, with large pecs and huge thighs. I could get lost in dreams about all the things those thighs could do to me.

"Fran?"

"Mmm?" I ask, realizing he must have said something before that.

"Then what *is* the point?"

"The point of what?" I ask, turning around to face him.

A rivulet of water breaks free from somewhere around his neck and trickles down over the bump of his left pec, along the indented line down the middle of his torso, and into the smattering of hairs that start at his navel and run all the way down into the boxers that sit snugly on his hips.

"Hello?"

Damn, I did it again.

"What?"

"What is the point of you being so upset about a dress you're never going to wear again?" he asks, with a hint of impatience.

"Can you put some clothes on?" I snap, spinning back around to look into the mirror.

"I have clothes on," he says, gesturing to his briefs. "But feel free to go and squelch your way around the mansion to find your keys if you're offended that I took off the wet suit I rescued you in."

"You didn't *rescue* me," I snort.

"Technically, I suppose you probably would've survived if I hadn't jumped in the lake. But that doesn't mean I didn't rescue you."

"Well thanks," I say, sounding very ungrateful even to my own ear.

"Any time," says Jonah, with an irritatingly smug grin.

I groan again, looking down at the ruins of my gown.

"I was supposed to sell it," I say.

"Sell it?" asks Jonah.

"The dress. Robbie said I could keep it. I was going to sell it on castoffcouture.com."

He stares at me in the mirror, blankly.

"It's a site where people sell second-hand designer clothes. But you still get a decent amount for them. Better than the auction sites or Craigslist or whatever, anyway."

"Ah," says Jonah. "Well, how much could you get for that thing anyway, even if it wasn't ruined?"

He's just a few feet behind me now and I stare at him in the mirror, aghast.

"That *thing*," I say, "is a one-of-a-kind gown from one of the most sought-after designers in the world right now. It's made of pure silk. The embroidery alone is a work of art."

He has that blank look on his face again, so I turn around to face him.

"Do you think every bride gets her maid of honor a dress like this?" I ask.

Jonah shrugs.

"No," I tell him. "The answer is no, they do not. Robbie got this for me so that she could tell me to keep it, knowing that I'd sell it." I can hear my voice rising in pitch but I can't stop it. "Because she knows I would never take money from her, and this is her way of making sure I can afford to live in the city to do an internship when I finish my exams in a few months."

I can feel a hot flush rising on my cheeks again and I feel like I might be about to cry right in his face, so I spin around yet again to look back into the mirror. Which is pointless, because there he still is, right behind me, staring at me in the mirror with a look of concern on his face. Or maybe it's pity.

I reach back to try and undo the gown, only to struggle with it as my fingers fumble about on some sort of pond slime.

"Stop," Jonah says, stepping closer. "Here."

He pushes my hand away and pulls the back of my dress upward and taught.

"Thanks," I say, trying to ignore the warmth of his fingers on my skin. I'm starting to shiver slightly from being so wet.

Based on every interaction I've ever had with Jonah, I fully expect him to make a quip about how he'll volunteer to get me out of my dress any time, but he doesn't.

"What exams are you doing?" he asks instead, leaning in to undo the hook and eye fastenings at the top of the dress.

"Uh. Accounting," I reply.

His fingers pause and he glances at me in the mirror. "Accounting?" he asks.

"Yes," I say, defensively. "What's wrong with that?"

"No, no. Nothing," he says, shaking his head. "Just... surprised."

"Why? Did you think I was going to work in the diner all my life?"

Not that there's anything wrong with that. Plenty of people who've worked in the diner with me will work there forever and they're amazing people. But aside from the copious amounts of time I spent in Robbie and Anna's house as a kid, my memories of Meadow Hill are not the happiest. I always had aspirations of leaving it behind one day. And now, looking at the state of my gown, that day seems much farther away.

"Never thought about it, really," says Jonah. At least he's honest. "But I know a lot of accountants and none of them are... you know."

He finally reveals the top of the zipper and slides it down, and I grab the front of the gown to keep it up.

"No," I say, turning around. "I don't know." There's an accusation in the way I look at him. But he's so close. The lake water didn't manage to wash away all his cologne and the masculine notes of sandalwood make me almost giddy. Or maybe that's the way he's looking down at me, intently, all but naked and barely half an arm's length away.

I could touch him if I wanted to. And he could touch me. And wouldn't that be completely clichéd, what with him being the best man and me being the maid of honor? I flick my gaze to his lips, and he reacts almost as though I shot lasers out of my eyes like some sort of swamp monster supervillain. He takes a big step back and away from me.

"Nothing," he says, shaking his head. "I'm going to shower."

He strides quickly for the bathroom, pointing toward the bed. "My phone's over there if you want to call Anna. I'll throw you some towels out."

∾

I was so certain I had everything packed. I even made a list and ticked everything off, one by one. I can even remember putting a little tick in the box beside "evening shoes." But as I stand in Jonah's room riffling through the bag that Anna brought me, I can suddenly remember the sound of the alarm tinkling away on my phone, telling me it was time to get my dad's meds ready, and putting the shoes down beside my luggage to go take care of it.

Anyway, the point is, I'm now wearing my lovely, dusky pink evening gown with luminous pink sliders that have "SUMMER HEAT!" sprawled across the top of them and little pictures of palm trees over the text.

"Interesting shoes," says Jonah with a smirk, when I go back into the sitting room area of his gigantic suite.

The good thing about consistently shitty luck is that it forces you to develop a sort of expectation that things will go wrong. It's hard to feel that bad about things you're expecting. *Expect nothing and never be disappointed*, as my father always says, before he's too drunk to speak.

"Thanks," I say, lifting my gown a little and sticking my leg out in front of me. I must look ridiculous, but Jonah made it clear earlier that he's not interested, so being dorky in front of him isn't going to do any harm. Heck, if I do enough of it, it might mortify me out of this ridiculous crush.

"Do me up?" I ask.

He looks up from my feet to my face, and I turn around and drag my hair over my shoulder.

"My zipper?"

"Oh," he says. "Sure."

He steps toward me and glances at me in the mirror, before looking down at my back. His cool fingers graze my skin as he pulls the sides of my dress together, and I suck my stomach in as far as I possibly can.

"There," he says.

I adjust the front of my dress, flick my hair back over my shoulder, and turn around.

"Thanks," I say, with a quick smile.

It's only then that I really take him in. The cologne I got a hint of earlier is all around me now, with him so close. He's wearing cream chinos, brown boat shoes and a white linen shirt with the sleeves rolled up to his elbows. I trail my gaze over him, from his toes up to his piercing blue eyes, only to find him doing the exact same thing to me.

His eyes flare a little wider when they meet mine like he's surprised to see me looking up at him. A crackling, electric sort of energy passes between us like lightning through chains. He lowers his gaze to my lips, licks his own, and reaches up to push a lock of hair out of my face.

The world feels like it's turning a little slower, but somehow my heart is suddenly racing faster, fluttering away in my chest while the tip of his thumb lingers a feather-light touch on my cheekbone.

The rap of knuckles on the door is so loud we both jump. Jonah seems to come immediately to his senses and takes a huge step backward and away from me, as though trying to get far enough away that whatever electricity was between us a moment ago couldn't possibly reach. He clears his throat and heads for the door.

"Guys?" Anna's voice is muffled through the door, but she goes on anyway. "Are you coming down to do your speeches? Or are you having sex? Because I've got a bet on with Tri—"

Jonah wrenches the door open. "Not," he says, holding a finger up to her. "Another word."

Anna grins at him and sticks her head into the room, looking over at me.

"Aw, man!" she says, and from my vantage point, I watch Jonah's right brow lift as he looks down at her, distinctly unimpressed.

Anna glances up at him, then does a double take, but in true Anna fashion, she is completely nonplussed by the scrutiny.

"Is everyone in the dining hall?" I ask.

Anna nods. "Yup! Just waiting for th—" she pauses as she looks at my feet, and I guess she feels guilty for laughing so hard at my mishap with the goose earlier because she just slides right on by the whole sliders situation without comment. "For the entrees. Robbie sent me to make sure you're alright."

I can just about feel my heart rate returning to normal after the almost-kiss with Jonah. "We're fine," I say. "Jonah let me use his shower because my keys are in your mom's purse. We'll head down in a sec."

"Alright," says Anna, glancing up to Jonah again and then back to me. "See you in a sec, then."

She turns around, her bridesmaid gown swishing around her, and heads back out.

Jonah watches her go for a second longer than is strictly necessary like he's avoiding looking back at me, and I notice him swallow before he looks back over to me. "Guess we'd better go on down," he says.

"Guess so," I say. "Is it alright if I ask one of the staff to come and get my bag from your room and take it up to mine later?"

He looks from me to my bag, which is neatly packed up and sitting beside the couch across the room.

"Sure," he says, and stands back a little, waving one arm cordially toward the door. "After you."

Chapter 2

One Year Later

"Fran!"

My workmate, Sarah, dashes in through the door and over to my desk. She's looking even more flustered than usual. "Have you seen the sales reports from last month? Jessica's on the warpath."

"Uh…" I stall, getting to my feet. I riffle through the document box on my desk marked "in", then through "out", just in case, and shake my head. "Nope. Has Tony got them?"

"Tony in Compliance?" she asks and doesn't wait for me to answer. "Maybe. Gotta go."

She rushes back out and I watch her leave. A second later, Jessica, my boss, comes marching in with her secretary, David, hot on her heels, taking frantic notes on his tablet with a stylus.

The best way to describe Jessica is that she's a powerful woman, in a powerful suit, doing a powerful job. I'm pretty much convinced that she only has one mode; immaculately presented and kicking ass, 24/7. I've tried to imagine what she'd look like relaxing in a pair of jeans and a t-shirt, mimosa in hand, but it's a bit like trying to imagine a handsome version of Harvey Weinstein. Impossible.

"Tell him I want it in my inbox by midnight tonight or he can find another job," she's saying as she enters the room. "And make sure I have a leads report by close tomorrow. Don't you have a meeting now?"

Since the stream of instructions has stopped, along with the click-click of her killer heels on the marble floor, I glance up and realize she's speaking to me.

"Oh," I say. "No. I was supposed to be minuting the accounting stand-up for you, but they canceled until tomorrow."

She doesn't even acknowledge that I've spoken, just keeps going, striding to her office and immediately redirecting to David.

"Get me a coffee. And find out where Sarah is with those sales reports."

Her office door slams and David stops and takes a deep breath, then sighs it out as he taps and drags his stylus across the screen of his tablet, presumably sorting the notes he's been taking into some sort of actionable list.

When he turns around, he glances over, gives me a brief, tight-lipped smile, and then quickly heads out the same way Sarah went, leaving me alone again.

I know what you're thinking. Why is an accounting intern working as a personal assistant to a middle manager at a marketing company? And it's a fair question.

This internship is one of the most sought-after in the city for trainee accountants. It doesn't pay particularly well, but I just about manage to get by between my salary and the money I got from eventually selling my bridesmaid dress. Whoever bought it paid way more than it was worth, given the state it was in after my unplanned dip in the lake. Like, *way* more. But I'm not complaining and I'm certainly not refunding. As long as I'm frugal, I'll get by. And next year, when "hell year"—Sarah told me this is what they call the year that new interns spend as Jessica's PA, which must suck for her, being Jessica's permanent PA—is over, I'll be able to choose which department I go into as long as I have the relevant education or skills. And this particular marketing company just happens to have one of the best accounting departments in the country. If I cut my teeth here, the world will be my lobster, as my mom used to say.

Jessica's door handle creaks down and I immediately sink into my chair, almost afraid of being caught in the same position I was in less than a minute ago when she last saw me. Jessica is a complete workaholic with an indomitable amount of drive. She's gunning for CFO when the position becomes available, and she expects everyone else in the entire world to be exactly like her. She opens her door just enough to poke her head through, and eyes me suspiciously.

"Are you off next week?" she asks, almost like an accusation.

"Yes," I say, standing up. "I cleared it with HR," I quickly add, feeling suddenly guilty about daring to take time off.

Jessica stares at me for a moment, and I fight the urge to apologize profusely for having the audacity to take time off and to offer to bring a sleeping bag with me tomorrow and just live in the office.

"Where are you going?"

"To the Bahamas," I say. "It's my best friend's wedding anniversary and they've invited everyone from the bridal party along to celebrate."

She eyes me. "You were a bridesmaid?" she asks, as though she can't believe it.

"Yes," I say with a nod. I was technically maid of honor, but I don't want to give her a stroke.

"And your friend is celebrating her wedding anniversary in the Bahamas?"

"Yes," I confirm.

"Aren't you from some town in the backend of bumfuck nowhere?" she asks.

This gets my hackles up. Partly because it comes up so often. Every other intern here is a city kid who thinks they're streetwise and worldly because they grew up in a gated community in a place that used to be interesting before it was gentrified.

"Yes," I say.

"Huh," she says, like she can't believe they let small town folk travel to the Bahamas.

"I even have a passport."

She doesn't get the sarcasm, thankfully. I tried a little sarcasm with her when I first started, to break the ice, and it did not go well. She walked in on me telling Sarah about a time I was in Chicago for a dinner with Robbie, and when she interjected to express her surprise that I'd ever been to Chicago, I told her that they occasionally bus people from small towns into cities so they can experience some culture. She told me it was a great idea and asked me a bunch of questions, which I had to invent answers to on the spot to avoid admitting that I was trying to be funny.

"Well make sure you get everything done before you leave," she says. "And catch up on everything when you're back."

"Of course," I say, nodding.

"And leave your phone number on your desk in case anyone needs to contact you."

There is so much I would say to this woman if I didn't need this internship so badly, but I've worked for years to get here and I'm not about to lose it because of one extremely overbearing, highly neurotic, borderline narcissistic manager. So, I smile sweetly and tell her that of course I'll leave my number on my desk and get everything done.

I barely manage to finish everything in my inbox by the time Robbie texts me to let me know she's outside. I pack all my things up and sling my purse over my shoulder, grab the handle of my suitcase, and head for the door. I'm almost there when I realize I've forgotten to leave my number, so I turn back and scribble it on a sticky note, press it down onto my desk, and then run for the elevator.

Robbie is waiting for me just outside the lobby, wearing jeans and a sweater and a big, wide smile. Between my internship and her book tour, it's been months since I've seen her. Given how Jessica feels about vacations, I haven't dared take any time off to visit Meadow Hill, the small town where Robbie and I grew up together, and where she now lives with Matt.

"Oh, wow," I say, dropping my suitcase for a moment to pull her into a tight hug. "Being a bestselling author really suits you, huh?"

Robbie laughs and looks me up and down. "Well, I could say the same about you and this place, Ms. Pants Suit," she says, and I roll my eyes.

"I'm trying to emulate my boss to get on her good side," I admit. I haven't had a chance to complain to Robbie *at length* about Jessica yet, so I'm very much looking forward to the next week. "She's a bit…"

"Fran?"

At the sound of my name, I turn around. Sarah is standing there, looking apologetically at me. She shoots a polite nod of acknowledgment towards Robbie… then does a double take and her jaw drops.

"Oh my God," she says, eyes practically leaping out of her head. "You're Roberta Sullivan!"

Robbie gives her a gracious, indulgent smile, all sparkling eyes and appled cheeks, and nods. "Yup, that's me."

"Wow. Oh, wow. I love *The King of Fury and the Queen of the Night*! I mean, I have read it like five times. I've got sticky notes and highlighter through the whole thing. I wish I had my copy with me for you to sign."

"Did you need something, Sarah?" I ask. I'm polite enough about it, but cocktails and gossip await so I need her to hurry it up.

"Oh, right. Yeah," she says, still sending fangirl glances Robbie's way. She holds up the sticky note I scrawled my number on. "Jessica says she can't read this. She sent me to get your number."

"It's in my HR file," I say flatly.

"Oh, come on, Fran," says Sarah, pleading. "You know what she's like. If I go up there without—"

"Tell you what," says Robbie, looping her arm through mine. "How about you go to HR and charm someone into giving you Fran's number from her file, and I will send my BFF back here with a signed trilogy for you after our vacation."

Sarah looks ecstatic, like she doesn't know what to pay attention to first. "Oh, my G—Yes! That's. BFF? I can't. Just brilliant. I love Trixian."

"And he'd love you," says Robbie, with practiced ease that betrays the months of book tours that are behind her.

"Wow," says Sarah, still looking starstruck. "I can't believe this."

"Was that it?" I ask—because cocktails await.

"Yes," says Sarah, still distracted. I'm like a disembodied voice to her now. Practically a ghost.

"Lovely to meet you, Sarah," says Robbie. "Have a great weekend!" She turns me around, grabs the handle of my pull-along luggage, and drags me off to her waiting limo, leaving Sarah near the door, shellshocked and speechless.

"There she is! How are you, Fran, my darling?"

I recognize the voice immediately as I climb into the back of the limo, and I dive across the car to wrap my arms around the neck of the middle-aged woman sitting there with a kind-eyed smile on her face.

"Brenda!" I squeal. "I didn't know you were coming! I mean, I knew you were coming to the island, but I figured you'd be on the boat."

Robbie's mom is not *technically* my mother, but after my mom died of cancer when I was eleven and my dad turned to the bottom of a bottle to cope, she became my mother in all but name.

"Hey, sweetheart," she says. "I've been calling every now and then but I know you're busy with your new job. How's it going?"

"Great!" I say. It's not really a lie. It'll be an amazing job next year. It's just right now that kinda sucks.

"Her boss is an asshole," says Robbie, getting in behind me.

"Well, that sounds *juicy*."

I recognize Anna's voice immediately. I hadn't even seen her sitting there, tucked in behind the door on the side of the limo I got in. I slide over and hug her.

"It's not, really."

"Is he mean to you?" asks Brenda with a dark expression, like she'd set the dogs on anyone who dared cross me.

"She... she's fine. Just a bit... you know."

"Of an asshole?" asks Anna.

"Yeah," I concede, nodding.

"Well, if she gives you any trouble let me know and I'll come and give her a piece of my mind," says Brenda.

"Mom, we're not in high school anymore," says Anna. "You can't just march in and go off on her boss like you did when Mr. Ashford called me an asshole."

"Well, I would," says Brenda, with a look of dead certainty on her face.

"Didn't you call him a dick first?" asks Robbie.

"Mr. Ashford?" asks Anna, shifting uncomfortably in her seat.

"Yeah. Actually, if I recall correctly, you told him he was becoming a bigger dickhead the further his hairline receded."

Anna glances sideways at Brenda, who is staring at her open-mouthed.

"Yeah," she admits.

Brenda gasps. "I gave that poor man hell, and you were asking for it!" she yells, and Robbie and I snort out a laugh at the same time.

"Well, I wasn't going to tell you I called my teacher a dick when I was fifteen!" Anna protests. "I was actually surprised he didn't tell you."

"Probably didn't have a chance," says Robbie. "You know what she's like when she gets going."

Brenda opens her mouth to respond, then closes it again, silently conceding. "I have terrible children," she says, looking at me. "They lie to me. And they let my glass run dry." She holds up a wine glass and waves it back and forth.

I sigh in commiseration, playing along. "Well, my best friend doesn't even give me a drink, to begin with."

"Alright, alright," says Robbie, still chuckling as she opens the mini bar and pulls out a bottle of something pale and bubbly, covered in little beads of condensation. "Time for a refill. Anna, grab Fran a glass. And don't drink too much or you'll get sick in the helicopter."

Not for the first time, I think to myself that being the best friend of a woman who made herself a ton of money *and* married a billionaire has its perks. I take the glass from Anna and hold it out to Robbie, who fills my glass first and then her mom's.

"To a wonderful vacation!" Robbie says, raising her glass. I lift mine alongside it, as do Brenda and Anna, and we clink them all together with a cheer. It's good to be back among family. I'm so happy to see them that I've already started to forget Jessica's scowling face.

Chapter 3

The sum total of my experience with boats is one trip on the Staten Island Ferry a few months ago when I first moved to New York City, and a duck-feeding stint on a paddle boat when I was about six years old. So when I say that I've never experienced anything like the yacht I'm traveling on with Robbie, I mean it. It has three floors, eight bedrooms, a sauna, a garage, and a hot tub. There's a huge living room, a beautiful sun deck, and staff on hand to meet your every need, whatever the time of day.

Despite living the billionaire lifestyle for a couple of years now, Robbie can't let go of her roots. She keeps invading the kitchen to prepare snacks and offering to fetch drinks for the staff on board.

I'm sprawled out on the sun deck when Robbie comes over and takes the lounger beside me. I can feel the sun's rays warming my skin through the thin layer of sunscreen I have on, and I'm sipping on some kind of non-alcoholic cocktail that one of the staff brought me.

"Hey," I say, smiling. "Where's Anna and your mom?"

"They're in the sauna," she says. "Anna found some internet video about the cardiac benefits of heat stress so she dragged mom down there."

I chuckle. "That sounds like her, alright."

We've been on board the yacht for about three days now. We're due to arrive at our destination sometime this afternoon, according to the captain. Flying would have been faster, but Robbie, Matt, Brenda, and Anna are all heading off on an extended vacation with the yacht after the anniversary party, and I'm glad for the extra time to just chill out and relax. Something about the open ocean has soothed my soul over the last few days, melting away all the worries and stress about work and life in general.

Which is more than I can say for Robbie, who I've caught staring out over the ocean with a worried look on her face more than once.

"So what's up?" I ask her.

"Hmm?" she says, looking over at me.

"Come on, you can't fool me. I've known you since you were five. Something's up. What is it?"

She stares at me and twists her lips to one side of her face, hesitating. It's just like Robbie to keep things to herself to avoid burdening anyone else, so I press her again.

"If you don't tell me, I'm going to tell Anna that you threw her favorite Doc Martens in the trash after you had that fight the week before prom."

"You wouldn't!" she gasps theatrically, and lies back on the lounger, chuckling. There's a short pause as she looks out to sea again, still hesitating, and then I can see the moment when she makes up her mind to tell me.

"Matt and I have been trying to get pregnant," she says.

"Oh, wow!"

"Yeah. I know I'm only 24, but we're lucky enough not to have the usual money worries, you know?"

I nod. Robbie is a bundle of love. Always has been—aside from the Doc Martens incident. Being a mother and loving a swarm of children is something I can't see myself doing for years, if ever—but her? It makes total sense for her.

"So why is that a problem?"

She looks out to the sea and shrugs. "Impatient, I guess."

"But not worried?" I ask.

"Not yet."

"Okay," I say. "But you know you can call me any time, right?"

Robbie smiles, the worry dissolving from her face as she looks over at me. "I do. Anyway, enough about me. How's dating life in the Big Apple?"

I snort. "Basically non-existent."

"No way?" she says, looking shocked.

Some women might take offense at the implication here, but it's a fair reaction. I've had many, *many* dates in my time. Mostly terrible ones with people I met on dating apps who were invariably looking for a one-and-done hook-up. And honestly? Nothing wrong with that, it's just not my thing. I like to know a little more about someone beyond their name and the fact that they can afford to go dutch at Olive Garden before I get hot and sweaty with them, y'know?

"I went on a few dates early on, but nothing for the last few months," I say. "No time. Work's crazy."

And money is super tight, but I don't tell Robbie that because she'll start scheming of ways to secretly give me money without seeming like she's trying to give me money, and I'd hate that.

I'm not bitter about her wealth and life. She's an amazing person and she deserves every penny she has and every ounce of happiness she can get. But every now and then I get this pang of realization, that we're the same age and she's married, successful, heading off on national book tours, and trying for a baby, while I'm living in a moldy shoe box in NYC, just barely starting my career with a low-paid internship, and terminally single. I'm not *resentful* exactly, but I do feel like I'm getting left behind sometimes.

"Will it be easier when you're done with the internship?" Robbie asks.

"Oh, yeah," I nod. "I mean, the work will be more chal-lenging, but that's a good thing. I'll be working toward accreditation, so it'll be progress, you know? This intern-ship is just the razor wire I need to crawl under to get there."

Robbie frowns at me. "That sucks," she says. "I mean they know you want to be an accountant. You aced every exam you ever took. It's just dumb to make you work as a PA for a year first."

"Jessica had to do it," I say. "So now everyone must. Everyone must be like Jessica."

"She sounds dreadful," says Robbie, for about the thirtieth time in the last three days. As I think I've already mentioned, I had a lot of pent-up complaining to do.

"Cheers to that," I say, lifting my glass and clinking it against Robbie's.

We arrive at the island in the late afternoon, just as the sun is lowering in the sky and casting a long, shimmering reflection on the crystal-clear Atlantic.

I don't know quite what I was expecting when Robbie said that Matt and Jonah joint-own a private island in The Exumas, but this place is absolute paradise. The water might be the bluest I've ever seen, and it laps lazily against the near-white sands of a beach that seems to go on forever. There's a dense forest of tropical trees just beyond the beach, and the pier where the yacht has docked leads to a sandy path that runs through the trees to a clearing with a beautiful white villa in the center. Some adults and children are playing on the beach, but I can't quite make out who they are from this distance.

"Wow," I breathe. Robbie, standing beside me, glances over with a grin.

I don't even bother to dress when we dock. I'm so excited to see the house that I just grab my drink, sling my phone purse over my head, shove my feet into my sliders, and step off the boat onto the pier.

"Oh, just a sec," says Robbie, turning back to the boat. "Go on ahead and I'll catch up. I want to grab the bag of toys Trish asked me to bring for the kids."

Trish is Robbie's sister-in-law, but she's known us way longer than Matt has. She and Matt's brother, Will, bought the café in Meadow Hill before we were even teenagers, and Robbie and I both worked for them; that old diner became our home away from home. I knew they were coming, but even still I get a little thrill of excitement at the prospect of seeing them.

I can barely take my eyes off the house as I walk along the pier. When I step down onto the sand, I stop and take a sip of my cool drink, just to marvel at the whole situation. Here I am, standing on a private island in the Bahamas, sun gently baking my skin, a cool drink in my hand, with nothing to do for almost a whole week.

"*Moooooooove!*"

I hear a voice—off to my right, loud and getting louder—and turn toward it, startling out of my daydream. It's accompanied by a chorus of children's giggles and whoops.

"Too late!"

It's Jonah, I realize, just before he dips, slams his shoulder into my waist, wraps his arm around my thighs, and lifts me. My drink goes flying off into the sand, and I feel a weird little shift around my torso.

"What the hell?!" I shout. "Jonah! Put me down!"

"I can't," he says, still running, as though I'm barely a burden to him. "It's a race!"

"Put me down!"

"Can't!"

I lift my head and look back along the beach, bobbing up and down with every stride he takes, to see a bunch of kids running after us, laughing. I recognize two of them as Zachary and Elliott, Will and Trish's children.

I grin at them and lift my arm to wave, and as they wave back, something catches my eye on the beach just beyond them. A scrap of material. Like a rag or a cloth has just been dumped there. It looks completely out of place in the pristine white sand. It's the same color as my bikini, and—

Oh, God. With a sudden pang of dread, I reach back and run my fingers across my bare back and realize that the scrap of cloth on the beach *is* my bikini. The top of it, anyway.

It dawns on me that I am being carried along the beach at speed, topless, with a bunch of kids running behind. My brain is still trying to calculate *precisely* how many ways this could go horribly wrong when Jonah lets out a triumphant yell.

"Winner!" he shouts and slows down.

"Jonah!" I shout. "Do not under *any* circumstances put me down!"

He stops completely. I can't see his face, but I can imagine the confusion on it.

"Huh?" he says, his breath coming in great big heaving gulps as he recovers.

"I've had a wardrobe malfunction. Don't move."

"What do you mean, Franchesca?"

"It's *Fran*," I say, with a note of irritation in my voice. "I lost my top."

The kids all start to arrive at the finish line, which I can now see scored into the sand below me, whooping and laughing. I grab tightly around Jonah's waist to make sure I don't end up leaving this island on some sort of offender register for indecent exposure.

"Oh, wow," says Jonah, sounding like he's spotted my top and realized what I'm talking about. He turns to the kids and shouts, "Last one to the house is a looooser!"

There's a sudden flurry of sand around Jonah's feet as the kids take off back toward the house, and as soon as they're gone he clears his throat.

"So what you're telling me," he says, as I cling onto him like an upside-down koala and cringe from the top of my toes to the bottom of my head, acutely aware of every inch of my skin that's touching his. "Is that those are your boobs pressing into my back?"

"You're ridiculous!" I hiss, and Jonah lets out a deep laugh that vibrates right through me.

"Don't be mean," he says, "or I'll make you walk back."

I open my mouth to speak and then think better of it. Walking down the beach with only my hands for coverage doesn't strike me as the ideal way to introduce myself to the other guests on the island.

"Just... take me to my top," I huff.

Jonah takes a leisurely pace back down the beach toward the pier, but just as my bikini top comes into view, he stops.

"Jonah!" I hear Brenda's voice. "How are you, young man?"

"I'm great, Mrs. Wilson," he says, casually, like there's nothing unusual about this whole situation at all. "So glad to have you on the island. We're going to have a blast."

"Yes, dear," says Brenda. "Uhm... is that Fran on your back?" she asks him.

I feel Jonah's head nod beside my hip. "Yup!"

"Hi, Brenda," I say, lifting my hand briefly from Jonah's belly to wave it at her. "I had a wardrobe malfunction."

Jonah dips down, basically shoving his butt in my face, and picks up my top from the sand. He shakes it out, sending a little cloud of sand to the floor.

"Ohhh," says Brenda, realizing what I mean. "I see. Well… can I help?"

"No, no," I say, feeling more and more ridiculous the longer this conversation goes on. And I'm starting to get a little lightheaded from being upside down. "If Jonah will just take me over to the trees I can fix it myself."

"Sure," says Jonah. "See you in a minute, Mrs. Wilson."

He turns around and heads for the forest of palm trees, his strong arms wrapped tightly around my legs to hold me in position.

"Here we are," says Jonah, and bends forward like he's going to set me down.

"Wait!" I call.

He freezes.

"Close your eyes."

"What?"

"Close your eyes! I don't want you to see my… breasts!"

Jonah snorts a laugh.

"Don't laugh," I say. "That's what they're called."

"I know," he says. "Just sounded funny, the way you said it."

I wobble a little on my feet as he puts me down and immediately slap my hands against my chest, but when I look up he has his head tilted upward and his eyes closed. I snatch my top out of his hand.

"Well, what would you call them? Knockers?"

A contemplative expression crosses his face, as though he's a sommelier considering a fine wine. "You don't really have knockers," he says. "That term is reserved for especially huge ones. Ditto for 'jugs.' In your case, I think I'd go with… 'bosoms.'"

I glare at him. "Well, you shouldn't be looking at my bosoms enough to be able to tell them apart from knockers or jugs in the first place!" I huff, as I shake the remnants of sand out of my top and start unraveling the strings.

"Says the girl who plastered them to my back."

"I did not *plaster* them to your back!" I protest.

"Oh, come on!" I can hear the smirk in his voice. "You were clinging onto me so tight it was like peeling off a velcro strip when I put you down."

"Oh my God!" I practically scream. "I do *not* have sticky melons!"

"Should have gone for titties there," he grins, and I can't help but let out a laugh.

"Sticky titties. Nice. Can you do me up?" I ask, turning my back to him.

"Well, that depends on whether or not I can look."

"You can open your eyes now," I tell him.

I hear a crackle underfoot as he steps forward through the branch-laced sand, and his fingers brush over mine as he gathers the strings of my bikini and pulls them together.

"How come I always end up dressing you?" he asks, as he pulls the knot taught. There's something in his voice that sends a ripple down my back and into my belly.

"You don't always end up dressing me," I say.

"True," he says. 'There was that one time I had to *un*dress you."

I feel a familiar pang of heat in my belly. I've dined on the memory of him sliding the zipper on the back of my dress down more times than I care to admit, so to have him just remember it like that is jarring.

"There," he says. "Done."

He drops the bow he's tied and I feel it brush against my back as it settles into place. I adjust my bikini and turn around.

"Thanks," I say, reaching back to tie the halter strings at the back of my neck. I do a couple of little jumps to make sure everything falls into place as it should, and stays there.

I notice Jonah's gaze travel downward as I do it, down over my newly affixed top and then quickly off into the thicket. He clears his throat. I figure the man who's constantly being photographed with a new supermodel on his arm is probably a little bit embarrassed about the slight jiggle of my belly when I jump, but whatever. We've already established his lack of interest, and I like pastries. A lot.

"Any time," he says and takes a long stride backward towards the beach. "We should go up to the house. Trish has been dying to see you guys."

At the mention of Trish, a broad grin spreads across my face and I march out of the trees ahead of him. "When did you arrive?"

"We flew in yesterday," he says. "Matt, Trish, Will, and me. And the kids and the extra staff, of course. And some supplies."

"In that?" I ask, pointing along the beach a little way to a second pier where a seaplane is floating idly, bobbing up and down on lapping waves.

"Yep," he says. "My pride and joy. It was a bit cramped, though."

"Oh," I say, frowning a little. "Well, will you have room for me on the way back? Robbie said you're flying me back to Manhattan because they're taking the yacht on vacation?"

Jonah nods, pacing along beside me. His skin is a golden tan and his sandy hair has sun-bleached highlights. He's taller than I remember, and broader, and since we've established that he's not at all interested in me, he's safe to ogle. So I do.

"It'll just be you and me on the way back," he says. "Will, Trish, and the kids are going with Matt and Robbie, and the extra staff will be helping to man the yacht since they'll mostly be at sea for the next couple of weeks."

"Oh," I say again. This is news to me. I had assumed that Will and Trish would be flying back with us, but it makes sense that they'd be heading off on vacation as well. I guess Georgia, one of the servers I used to work with, is looking after the café for them.

"Don't worry, Franchesca," he says. I decide to just let the full-name thing slide. "I'm a pretty good pilot."

We're almost at the villa now, and I see a figure emerge from the front door and start jogging towards us with an excited squeal. It's Trish, wearing a smile almost as big as my own. She spreads her arms while she's still ten feet away, and I pull her into a big hug.

"Trish! I've been so excited to see you," I say. "How are you?"

"Pfft," she says. "Are you kidding? I'm amazing. Look at this place!"

She has a point. The villa is even more beautiful up close than it was from the beach.

"Come on," Trish grins, looping her arm through mine. "Will's been dying to see you."

I let her lead me along, only glancing over my shoulder just as we reach the door of the house. Jonah is still standing at the end of the path, looking up at us. He turns away quickly as our eyes meet, and gazes off down the beach.

Chapter 4

The house on the island is beautiful. Call me prejudiced, but I didn't expect so much taste in a house owned by two straight men. Every room has a theme, and it changes just a little as you walk through, giving it an understated coherence. The entire wall of the sitting room opens out onto the veranda and deck, and everything is clean and crisp, with tasteful accents here and there.

My room is spectacular. It's gigantic, with double doors that lead outside and a huge super king bed. The ensuite bathroom is a wet room with a rainfall shower in the middle, slightly set off from the drain, and candles and towels have been laid out beside the wash basin. There's even a jug of water and a small box of chocolates on each of the two nightstands beside the bed. Which sort of rubs my face in the fact that I'm one of a vanishingly small number of single adults currently on the island, but what's a girl to do?

More people will be arriving for an overnight stay in a couple of days, anyway. Maybe one of them will be a tall, handsome, golden-tanned, blue-eyed Adonis with a penchant for interns who like flan.

I pull my dress on over my head and settle it in place. It's a vibrant orange number that falls to my knees, sleeveless, with a gathered bust. I glance at the strappy-heeled sandals I brought with me, but I decide I'll keep those for the party instead, and shove my feet into my sliders before heading out to the deck.

Aside from the kids, who are inside playing board games, everyone on the island is already out here, sprawled along a comfortable U-shaped couch around a central table. The table is laid with bottles of wine in ice buckets and a huge selection of charcuterie-style boards, some brimming with cheese and meats, some with fruits, and others with crusty rolls of fresh-baked bread. It looks heavenly, and I suddenly realize that I'm starving.

"Here she is!" says Matt, as I stroll out. It's the first time I've seen him since I arrived. He's been off around the island all day, making sure everything is perfect for the anniversary. Robbie's a lucky girl.

"Hi!" I grin, as he pulls me in for a hug. "How's my favorite billionaire?"

"Hey!" calls a familiar voice. I turn around to see Jonah giving me a playful scowl from the other side of the table.

"What?" I ask.

He feigns a wounded expression. "After all we've been through together, I'm not even your favorite billionaire?"

Anna's eyebrows shoot up, and a big grin spreads across her face. "I *knew* you two did it at the wedding!" she says smugly.

"You did?" asks Trish, wide-eyed.

"We did not!" I say. "Anna, shut up. Jonah, kindly tell Anna that we did not 'do it at the wedding.'" I can feel a flush seeping up out of the front of my dress as I stare daggers across at him.

"We did not," confirms Jonah. "I'm kidding."

I shoot Jonah one final look—a look that says "don't you even dare *think* about telling the velcro boobs story"—and then I take a seat right between Robbie and Trish.

The next few hours pass full of laughter and old stories, and I love every second of it. Despite the fact that I've spent every moment since my mom died planning to leave Meadow Hill, I adore these people and their warmth and the love they so generously give. They are family in every sense of the word.

I'd go to Robbie's house for a playdate once a week when I was a kid, but when my mom got sick and needed to go to the hospital all the time, it was Brenda who took me in while my dad watched the love of his life wither away to a husk of skin held together with tubes and tape. It was Brenda who held my hand through the funeral when my dad was consumed with grief. And when she dropped me home one day and saw the way my dad swayed in the doorway while he slurred out his thanks, it was Brenda who told Robbie I could sleep over any night and come on every family vacation. She even tried to get him to quit drinking a few times, but the rehab never lasted.

I don't blame him. Every picture in his house is him and my mom in some different place, at some different time, being madly in love with each other ever since high school. The trauma of losing her broke him. It is what it is. But when she saw the broken pieces of me, it was Brenda that carefully picked them up one by one and slowly glued them back together, and it was Robbie and Anna who treated me like a third sister without question or reserve.

When night starts to fall, Trish and Will disappear to put the kids to bed, and Robbie and Matt head out for a walk along the beach. Brenda and Anna start their usual argument about Anna's career choices, with Brenda trying to convince Anna to go back to college while Anna insists that her miniature painting business really can take off.

"Crafting is not a life plan," says Brenda, obviously struggling to keep her voice even, and I take that as my cue to get up and find somewhere else to be before either side tries to rope me in for support.

I decide to take a closer look around the house, out of sheer curiosity. Every room I walk into lights up automatically as I enter. There's a large lounge beyond the sitting room, and beyond that, a fully-equipped fitness room. I round the corner to a huge kitchen, which seems to be mostly for show since there's another kitchen the staff use to prepare food on the other side of the house. Beyond that are a huge pantry and a wine cellar that's bigger than my whole apartment, fully stocked with hundreds of bottles.

Once I cross through the kitchen, I start seeing parts of the house that aren't just bigger, better versions of things in normal-people houses. There's a cinema, for starters, with big, fluffy recliner chairs and a popcorn machine in the corner. Next, I walk into a smaller room that has a big, cushion-covered couch in it, where the walls are bookshelves all around. It immediately makes me think of Robbie, and I take a moment to look through the collection. I smile to myself when, sure enough, right there in the correct alphabetical slot, I find *The King of Fury and the Queen of Night*, by Roberta Sullivan.

Through the door on the far side of the library, I find myself in a corridor. The wall on one side is made entirely of glass, through which I can see a large outdoor swimming pool, hot tub, sauna, and lots of sun loungers.

I stand still for a moment, mesmerized by the rippling patterns on the pool's surface until the quiet notes of a slow, sad jazz tune catch my ear. I head down the corridor and around a corner, tilting my head now and then to follow the music until I find myself standing in front of a nondescript wooden door.

I push the handle down slowly and ease the door open, looking inside. This room is a dark, moody bar, all old wood, red velvet, and low lighting. It reminds me of an old saloon. I instantly love it.

I don't even notice Jonah, sitting in the shadowed corner at the far end of the bar, until he turns around in his seat to face me.

"Oh," I say, not quite sure what to do. I feel like I've been caught snooping in someone's home—which is basically exactly what's going on—and I start to back up. "Sorry."

"Stay," he says.

I freeze for a moment, still unsure what to do.

"Whiskey?" he asks, plucking the bottle from the bar beside him. There's a glass in front of him with a little amber liquid at the bottom. Something about this man who has it all sitting in his own private bar, drinking alone as a melancholy blues song drifts slowly through the air, piques my curiosity.

"Sure," I say, closing the door behind me. "Can't let you drink all alone, can I?"

He rises from his stool to his full height and indicates a round table in the middle of the room, surrounded by four plush chairs. He's wearing a pair of cream shorts, a white linen shirt with short sleeves, and some blue sliders. He looks great, and when he moves I get a waft of his sandalwood-scented cologne that takes me right back to that mansion room in Florida.

"Can't have a 'lil lady propping up the bar," he says, in what I guess is his best take on a deep Southern drawl. It's terrible, and the grin he gives me says he knows it. "It wouldn't be proper, ma'am."

"Well now," I say, in my equally awful attempt at the same. "I was fixin' to go to my bed, but don't mind if I do, Mr. Wells."

Jonah chuckles, puts a glass down in front of me, and pours a two-finger measure of whiskey into it before he takes a seat opposite me.

"Try it," he says and takes a small sip from his own glass.

I pick the glass up and throw it back, shuddering as the liquor works its way down my gullet.

"Whew," I say. "It burns."

Jonah doesn't say anything. I look over at him and he's staring at me, open-mouthed, eyes wide.

"What?" I ask.

"I…" he says, and then closes his mouth, speechless. "Wait there."

He rises from his seat again, goes to the bar, and rummages around. I sit up in my seat, craning my neck as he ducks behind the bar. When he comes back, he's carrying a different glass, shaped a bit like a tulip. It's almost a champagne flute, but with a short, thick bottom.

"Okay," he says, placing the glass down in front of me. He spreads his legs, reaches between them, and pulls his chair forward toward me until he's so close I can practically feel the heat of his body.

"So, this whiskey is from Scotland. It's single malt."

"What does that mean?" I ask.

"Single malt? Just means that it was distilled once in one distillery. Double malt is a mix of two single malts."

"'Kay," I say, watching him pour a measure.

"Alright," he says. "First you need to nose it."

He picks up the tulip glass and brings it just in front of my face.

"Like, just stick my nose in there?" I ask.

Jonah nods, so I oblige.

"Inhale deeply," he says, his voice quiet and smooth. "They didn't mature it sixteen years so you could throw it back like tequila."

I glare at him sidelong, but before I can say anything, he cuts me off. "Inhale."

After a moment, he pulls the glass away.

"Smells like whiskey," I say with a shrug.

"You need to do it three times," he says.

"Why?" I ask. "Will I get bad luck if I don't? Is it like some superstition?" I affect my best Scottish accent—which is about the worst you can imagine. "Ye who do not

44

sniff three times shall be accursed to live forever in misery!"

I grin at him, and though he shakes his head in exasperation, his eyes are sparkling and he can't quite keep the smile off his face. "No," he says. "Your nose needs time to pick up the notes. Trust me. On the third try, assuming your nose works, you'll start to pick up some floral scents. Maybe a little nuttiness. I get a hint of raisin from it as well, but just very subtly."

I narrow my eyes at him, skeptically, but I give him a nod. He brings the glass to my face again, and I put my nose inside.

"Still whiskey," I say when he pulls it away.

"I said three," he says, swirling the deep amber liquid in the glass. He brings it back again after a short break, and I lean forward to inhale.

My eyes widen and I look sideways at him. It still smells of whiskey, but sure enough, there's a floral undertone, that hint of nuttiness he mentioned, and even a very light note of raisin. In an instant, he turns into a human-shaped ball of pure smugness.

"Told you!' he says, excited as a kid on Christmas morning.

"Yeah, yeah," I say. "Fine. I can smell raisins. But they don't sell whiskey just so people can sniff it."

"Correct," he says. His excitement is almost palpable. You wouldn't even think it was possible for this guy to sit in a darkened room and drink alone. He inches forward on his chair even more, his thigh pressing against my knees.

"So now that you've nosed it, you taste it," he says. He brings the rim of the glass to my lips, and much to my surprise, I feel his other hand come to rest gently on the back of my head.

"Close your eyes," he whispers.

I don't even try to argue. The heat of his inner thigh warming my knees is sending ripples right up my spine, and my scalp tingles under his touch. Every nerve ending in my body is coming to life all at once, and it only gets more intense when I close my eyes and let my head rest back against his hand.

He tips the glass against my lips, and my mouth fills with a wash of warmth.

"Don't swallow," he whispers.

The fifteen-year-old boy who lives in the deepest recess of my brain comes suddenly to life, and I try and fail to restrain a snort. I accidentally inhale the whiskey and the burn is immediate and harsh. I swallow quickly, then burst forward, half-coughing, half-laughing.

"What?" asks Jonah, his head tilted in bemusement.

"Nothing," I say quickly, not wanting to explain, but also not able to wipe the grin off my face.

"Well, something's tickled you," he says.

"It's childish."

"Tell me."

"It's the first time a man's ever told me not to swallow."

Jonah grins at me, shaking his head and rolling his eyes. I notice his Adam's apple bobbing up and down as he chuckles. He really is just stupendously handsome when he smiles. It's no wonder all the hottest models go for him.

"Okay, okay," I say, my grin finally dropping. I close my eyes, tip my head back, and open my mouth. "Try again."

Nothing happens. Opening one eye, I look over at him. He seems lost in thought all of a sudden.

"Jonah?"

"Right," he says, then clears his throat and shakes his head. "Okay, so this time, just let it wash over your tongue, underneath it, swirl it around your mouth, and let your palate do its thing."

I feel the cool rim of the glass on my lips. It feels so intimate, suddenly. His thigh presses against me a little harder when he leans forward. I'm drowning in the smell of him and the warmth of him and the tingle all over my body, and the featherlight pressure of the glass on my mouth sends a bolt of long-neglected need down my body. I can feel goose pimples prickling my skin, and I'm acutely aware that Jonah can probably see them.

My mouth floods with whiskey again, but this time, I manage to hold it just like Jonah told me to. I swirl it around my tongue.

"That's it," he whispers. "Just like that. Caress it with your tongue."

I roll my tongue up and down, side to side, exploring the tingling heat with every tastebud.

"You'll get those same floral notes," he says, and I pick them up right away. "Some spices and plum."

I nod, and the "Mmhmm," I hum comes out like a salacious moan.

I hear him swallow again, and his voice is a little lower when he speaks again. "The plum is from the sherry that was matured in the barrels before they were used for the whiskey," he says.

His fingers move on the back of my head, ever so slowly, fanning out and then in, gently massaging my scalp and lulling me into a state of deep relaxation with a side of heady arousal.

"You might be able to taste the oak of the barrel, too," Jonah says.

I nod, unable to speak. My mind is suddenly too addled to find words. I'd never admit it to anyone, but I wish he'd just kiss me. And pluck me out of this chair and do things to me on the bar.

When he speaks again, he's closer. So close I can feel his breath on the shell of my ear. His voice is barely more than a whisper.

"Now swallow it."

I feel a deep pang of clenching need in my belly at the sound of those words. I have no idea how this became so erotic, but I think whiskey is my new favorite drink. Good-bye, bellinis. It was fun while it lasted, but you never made me pant.

I swallow, and Jonah removes his hand from the back of my head.

"Now breathe through your nose," he says. "A little through pursed lips, too. You'll get a finish of spice and fruit."

As though my tastebuds are entirely under his command, I instantly taste every note he mentions, while the warmth of the alcohol burns gently at my throat and spreads through my chest.

"Okay," I say, and my voice crackles on the first syllable. I open my eyes and look at Jonah, who is staring at me intently. "I admit, that tastes good."

One side of his mouth lifts in a smile. His gaze drops to my lips, and for a moment I think I might be about to have a vacation fling with a billionaire. And then I remember that Jonah can blow hot and cold faster than my Dyson Airwrap.

"You have a little whiskey just…" He reaches up and places his fingertips at my jaw, and runs his thumb along the very corner of my mouth.

My heart jumps as he locks eyes with me. His thumb keeps going, running a torturously slow path along my lower lip. His tongue darts out and wets his lips, and he starts to lean forward toward me.

"Fran?"

Robbie's voice calls from the other side of the door, muffled but unmistakable.

Jonah's chair screeches against the wooden floor as he retracts his hand and pushes away from me like I'm suddenly white-hot and/or poisonous. I reach up and pat the back of my head where he was massaging my scalp to smooth down my hair.

"In here," I call.

I look at Jonah, but he's not meeting my eye. He shuffles his chair a little farther away from me, and I know instantly that we're back in "cold" territory.

"Hey," says Robbie. She pauses for a moment, looking from me to Jonah and back again.

"Hey," I say. "I found Jonah drinking whiskey so I decided to join him. You want a drink?"

Jonah turns around to look toward the door, a breezy smile on his face, as though a mask has slipped neatly back into place.

"It's good stuff," he says.

"No, thanks," says Robbie. "I just came to check whether Fran's room is OK." She lowers her voice conspiratorially. "Dale and Liam just arrived and everyone else is coming tomorrow, so I want to make sure you have the room you want before I let them pick one."

Dale is Matt's secretary, and Liam is his husband. I've met them a few times in Meadow Hill.

"My room's great," I say, chuckling at her. "I took the one that sort of sticks out on the East so I can get the morning sun."

"Alright," she says. "I'm going to get Dale and Liam settled and then hit the hay."

"Okay," I say. "Goodnight!"

"Oh, by the way," she says, stopping on her way out the door. "You two are paired tomorrow for the games."

"Games?" I say, glancing at Jonah, who looks suddenly pale.

"We run games whenever we have parties here. They're fun," Jonah says. His expression suggests otherwise.

"What sort of games?" I ask.

"You'll see!" says Robbie, grinning. "But since Jonah is already rich enough to buy whatever he wants, and you're technically his guest, I guess if you guys win the prize it can all go to you, Fran. Right, Jonah?"

Jonah looks from Robbie to me. "Sure," he says with a shrug.

"What sort of prize?" I ask, a little more interested now.

"You'll see!" repeats Robbie.

A thick arm appears around her waist, and a moment later, Matt's head pops over her shoulder.

"Hey, bro," says Matt, looking over at Jonah. He does the same thing Robbie did, glancing at me and then back to Jonah and letting a silent question hang in the air.

"Hey," replies Jonah. He holds up the bottle and tilts it from side to side in the air. "Drink?"

"Nope," says Matt. "I'm taking my beautiful wife to bed. Goodnight!"

With that, he wraps his other arm around Robbie's waist, lifts her off her feet, and carries her backward out of the room while she giggles.

The noise fades away as the door clicks closed, and Jonah and I sit in awkward silence for longer than is comfortable. I wonder if he's also mentally contrasting Matt and Robbie's easy love and affection with whatever this weird on-off tension is between us, that always seems to end with us walking as quickly as we can away from each other.

"Well, it's late," Jonah says, getting to his feet. If he was melting heat a few minutes ago, this is its polar opposite. He's cool, calm, and collected. I almost feel like we just had a business meeting.

I'm tempted to shake his hand. *Thank you, Mr. Wells. We did great work today.* Instead, I nod and slip into business mode myself, standing up and smoothing down my dress.

"Thanks for the whiskey," I say, suddenly desperate to be absolutely anywhere else.

"Yeah, sure," he says. He looks from me to the glass on the table. His gaze lingers on it a moment, and then he reaches to pick it up, along with the other glasses and the half-full bottle. "At least you know how to drink it properly now."

I'm pretty sure that if I ever try to drink whiskey like *that* in public, I'll be arrested. But I just let out a weak chuckle and say, "Yeah. Okay, goodnight!"

Jonah doesn't even turn around to look at me. He heads towards the bar, calling "Goodnight" over his shoulder at me. I push open the door and step out into the corridor, letting it click shut behind me.

Despite only drinking two mouthfuls of whiskey, my head feels fuzzy and I need some air before bed. Rather than traipsing back through the house and risk having to make small talk with anyone I meet along the way, I slip out of the door beside the pool and lay down on one of the sun loungers to think.

Chapter 5

I've decided to just be friendly acquaintances with Jonah and to make sure he knows it. I was never looking for a life-long commitment from him anyway, but the hot and cold thing is driving me nuts. He's an attractive guy and a fling would have been nice, but quite frankly I could do without the *possibility* of a fling being repeatedly dangled in front of me like a carrot only to end up with the stick every time. It's starting to make me feel desperate, and I don't like it.

I arrive at the beach with Robbie, ready for the games. She's still staying tight-lipped about them, wearing sneakers as she advised everyone at breakfast this morning. Everyone else is already here, so I slip off to find Jonah since I already know we'll be together. *Partnered* together, I mean. For the games. Friendly acquaintances!

"Howdy, partner," I say, thumping Jonah's upper arm with my fist.

He looks down at the spot on his arm that I hit, then up to my face. His eyes are a little bloodshot and he has a five o'clock shadow at 10 am. He looks suspiciously like he had a late and drunken night.

"Don't be loud," he says, flatly. His voice is full of gravel.

"Awww. Hungover?" I ask.

He frowns at me, his lips pressed into a thin line.

"Alright, everyone!" shouts Matt. Robbie is beside him, rummaging in a large box. "Welcome to the very first annual anniversary games."

There's a little ripple of applause, and Jonah winces.

"Here," I say, passing him the bottle of water I've brought with me.

"Thanks," he says, almost reluctantly, but he takes the bottle from me and starts chugging.

"Now you'll be paired off into four teams," says Matt. "Trish and Will, you're together."

Trish and Will high-five each other.

"Hey, go easy," I whisper to Jonah, as he continues to guzzle my water.

"Dale and Liam, team two."

"We're so going to win!" says Dale, and Liam gives him a little shove.

"Team three is my wonderful mother-in-law and my wife's sister."

Everyone chuckles, apart from Jonah, who's still chugging on my water, and Anna, who pokes her tongue out at Matt.

"And team four," says Matt.

"Oh my god, will you *stop*!" I say, a little too loud.

There's a slightly awkward silence, followed by a quiet sucking sound as Jonah separates my water bottle from his lips and lets out a satisfied, "Aaah."

Matt pauses for a second, looking a little bemused. "Team four, Fran and Jonah!"

"I can't believe you drank half my water!" I hiss, grabbing the bottle back from him,

"Cooperation is the name of the game today," says Matt.

I catch Anna looking over at Jonah and me and snorting a laugh.

"Don't worry, I'll fill it up before we start," Jonah whispers.

"Uh, hello? We've *already* started."

He doesn't look like the water's done him any favors. He's wearing what looks to be a permanent frown, and he reaches out and places his hand over my mouth.

"Shh," he says.

I press my lips together behind his hand, then shove it away.

"We're doing a scavenger hunt," says Matt.

Jonah groans.

"But that would be too easy."

"It wouldn't," Jonah says under his breath, bending a little closer to my ear. "This guy doesn't know what easy is. One year, he basically made everyone do a triathlon. The CEO of a well-known marketing company almost drowned, 20 meters out to sea. I had to take a jet ski out to rescue him."

"So, one out of each pair will be wearing a blindfold," Matt continues. Robbie starts handing out blindfolds to each team.

"I'm not being blindfolded," says Jonah, quickly, looking resolute with his arms folded over the wide expanse of his chest.

"Well, I don't want to be blindfolded either."

"I'll vomit," he says, and given the state he's in, I figure he's not joking. I sigh with resignation and take the blind-fold from Robbie.

"You may take the blindfolds off for rest breaks, but only when you're stationary," Matt calls. "If any of the spotters —that's Robbie, me, and the kids—find you without your blindfold when you're on the move, you'll be disqualified."

"So we can just not put it on and go back to bed?" asks Jonah.

"No, you can't," says Matt. There's something in the smile he gives Jonah that perplexes me. They usually dig at each other constantly, in a joking, brotherly sort of way, but this smile is kind, almost sympathetic. And Matt moves on quickly instead of having a jab at Jonah for his hungover state. Something is definitely up.

"There are seven clues, and seven tokens you need to bring back with you. Like this," says Matt, pointing to Robbie, who's holding up a small, metal disc, about the size of a hockey puck. "If nobody gets seven, then the team with the most will win. If two or more teams get the same number of tokens, then the team that gets back here first wins."

"What if there's a tie?" calls Anna.

"In the unlikely event that there's a tie, meaning two teams arrive back at exactly the same time with the same number of tokens," says Matt, "then we'll have a tiebreaker event tomorrow."

"More importantly, what's the prize?" shouts Will.

"Ah, good question," says Matt.

I'm curious to see what the prize is. The most I've ever seen won at one of these events was a $100 voucher for a theme park, donated by the theme park, and I thought that was pretty swanky at the time.

Matt turns around and waves to a member of staff who's standing on the yacht a short distance away; a young guy about my age called Roberto, who traveled with us to the island. He gives Matt a nod and reaches down.

A moment later, the yacht's cargo hold whirrs slowly open and reveals a shining, black and silver motorcycle.

I gasp, and I'm not the only one.

Will is obviously imagining himself rolling down the freeway on it. Brenda is seeing a million different images of Anna mangled on the roadside. But me? All I can see are dollar signs. That bike could be the difference between spending the rest of this year financially stressed or knowing I can easily cover all my bills.

"How much is that worth?" I ask Jonah.

When I look up, he's staring at the bike, almost salivating. My mind casts back to the first time I ever met him, back when Robbie still lived with her mom in Meadow Hill and Matt had camped outside her house (literally!) in a bid to win her over. Jonah had arrived on his bike, looking absolutely panty-wettingly amazing in leathers, and flirted outrageously with me at the door. It's a pattern, I guess.

Jonah looks down at me, stares at me for a moment as though his brain is trying to catch up to what I just said, and then he shrugs. "About fifty grand? Maybe sixty?"

I sputter, looking back at the bike.

"And how many of those do you already have?" I ask Jonah.

"How many of that *particular* bike?" he asks. "Or how many Harleys?"

"Oh," I say. "Is that a Harley Davison?"

Jonah stares at me like I'm a different species for a moment.

"I have three Harleys. Zero of that model."

"Is it a good one?" I ask.

"I mean, look at it," he says, pointing at the bike as though I might not have seen it yet. "It's beautiful."

I don't see the appeal, myself. Until Jonah speaks again.

"If we win, I'll buy it from you for sixty."

"Sixty *grand?*" I hiss, looking up at him.

He looks down at me, and I see the realization dawn on his face that maybe, somewhere in the world, to some person, that amount of money might be a lot. Maybe even right here and right now, and to the person standing in front of him.

"Sure," he says. "Unless you're not selling?"

"I'm selling!" I say quickly. That much money will make me relatively comfortable for the duration of this hellish year of my internship, and I can feel determination solidifying in my gut.

"The starting horn will be blown in…" Matt looks at his watch. "Ten minutes!"

"Okay," I say to Jonah, grabbing him by the arm. "Come with me. I'm not losing that Harley Davison just because you can't hold your liquor."

Jonah winces harder than anything his hangover has thrown at him this morning. "Please stop calling it a Harley Davison," he pleads, genuinely anguished. "Please. It's *Davidson*. Harley *Davidson*."

I drag Jonah back up the house and force him to eat two eggs, a banana, and some crackers while I refill my water bottle. He doesn't protest about it too much. He actually looks a bit better by the time we're back on the beach.

Matt directs everyone with a blindfold to put them on; that's Anna, Will, Dale, and me. And then, with a theatrical flourish, he opens an envelope and reads out the first clue.

"You'll find the strongest current here. Head for the morning sun." He repeats it, and I can hear whispering from the other teams as they confer.

Matt blows the air horn, and Jonah immediately sets off up the beach, dragging me along behind him.

"You know where we're going?" I ask, concentrating hard on walking blindfolded through the soft sand. It's not as easy as you'd think.

"Powerhouse," he says. "Strong current—electricity. And it's on the East end of the island, where the sun rises."

"Ooh, clever," I say.

After a few minutes, I feel my skin start to cool, and the ground begins to crackle beneath my feet.

"Where are we going?" I ask.

"Into the trees," Jonah says. "Liam and Dale were tailing us, so we'll cut through and lose them."

"Are you always this competitive?" I ask.

"Pretty much."

"I guess that explains the billions, huh?"

"Pretty much," he says again, giving me the distinct impression that I'm just distracting him from his mission.

He doesn't speak again for a few minutes, and I aimlessly follow wherever he leads me, trying not to linger on the feeling of his big hand wrapped around mine.

"Fallen tree," he says, stopping.

"Huh?"

His hands land suddenly on either side of my waist, and he lifts me from the floor. I instinctively reach out and grab at his shirt to steady myself. He turns, takes a big step, and sets me down again.

"There was a fallen tree," he says, taking my hand again and carrying on.

"Oh. Thanks."

"No problem, partner," he says, echoing my greeting from this morning.

I don't try to make any small talk. In part because it's a difficult thing to do when you can't see your interlocutor, and in part, because I can't think of much that a very hungover person on a reluctant but nonetheless very determined mission would want to hear. So I just trail behind Jonah in silence, letting him lead me, obediently stepping over objects when he directs me to and letting him lift me over the ones that are too difficult to navigate.

I'm not sure exactly how much time has passed when I start to feel the sun on my skin again and stop hearing the sounds of cracking leaves and twigs underfoot, since the monotony of walking without seeing becomes a sort of Zen meditation after a while. I'd guess it's about twenty minutes before Jonah finally comes to a standstill without giving me any directions or lifting me over any fallen trees. Since we've stopped, I decide to take off my blindfold and see where we are.

"No peeking when you're walking!" Zachary's voice is familiar, and once I've removed the blindfold and blinked away the sting of the sudden light, I can see him and Robbie come into view, obviously policing the first stop on the hunt.

"Are we in the lead?" I ask Robbie.

She nods. "Yup. By a long way, it looks like."

I look back down the beach and I can see Anna and Brenda, no more than little specks in the distance.

"What about Liam and Dale?" I ask.

"I saw them disappear into the trees right behind you two," says Robbie. "But they haven't shown up yet."

I glance up at Jonah and he's wearing his trademark smug expression.

"Yeah, yeah," I say. "I already said it was clever."

"Got our next clue?" Jonah asks, turning to Robbie.

"Yes," she says, and reaches into a fanny pack she has around her waist. "And your token."

She hands them both over to Jonah and turns to me. "Don't forget to put your blindfold back on before you leave, or Zachary will report you."

"I will," confirms Zachary, looking deadly serious.

"The place where today comes before yesterday," says Jonah, reading out the clue.

"Hmm," I say, tapping my chin.

"Like a time zones thing?" asks Jonah, looking over at Robbie, who just smiles sweetly and shrugs her shoulders.

"Oh, I know!" I say, as it suddenly dawns on me. "It's the words. The dictionary. T comes before Y."

Jonah looks to Robbie for confirmation, and she gives him a very subtle nod.

"Clever girl," says Jonah, quickly wrapping the blindfold back around my head without warning. In any other context, I might just die on the spot if a tall, handsome guy was blindfolding me and calling me a clever girl. But this is just me and my friendly acquaintance buddy doing a scavenger hunt. Nothing to see here, folks. Move along.

Jonah grabs my hand and pulls me back along the beach toward the house. "There's a big dictionary in the reading room back at the house," he says, and picks up his pace.

∼

About five clues in, as we're looking for the sixth and seem to be way ahead of everyone else, the inevitable finally happens; my luck turns bad. We're traipsing through the forest—again—when my foot catches on a branch and my ankle twists just enough to make me gasp. As soon as he hears it and sees me limping along behind him, Jonah takes the blindfold off and directs me to sit on a nearby rock, while he crouches down and pulls my leg toward him.

"We're way ahead, by the looks of it," he says. "We can afford to take a break."

"Okay," I concede, as he pulls the sneaker off my injured foot. "But not too long."

"You really want that money, huh?"

"Uh… duh," I say, looking at him like he's crazy. "We're not all billionaires, you know. Some of us are interns on paltry wages, struggling to rent a shoebox apartment in a super shady part of New York City."

"Point taken," he says, kneading the bottom of my heel. "Is it the internship you wanted?"

I'm actually shocked that he remembered our conversation back at the wedding, a year ago. So shocked that I don't respond for a moment—long enough that he apparently feels the need to clarify.

"The one you sold the fancy gown for?"

Okay, so this guy actually pays *way* more attention to the things I say than I had previously imagined.

"Yeah," I say.

A broad smile breaks out on his face. "Good job."

I search his face for any hint of sarcasm, but I can't find any.

"Thanks. I got lucky, really. Someone bought that pond-stained gown for way more than it was really worth. Almost as much as it cost new. Otherwise, I'd be living in a cardboard box instead of a slightly bigger box made of bricks."

Jonah shifts his hand on my foot and doesn't look up. I guess he's not that interested in dresses, or the ins and outs of the second-hand couture market. And the twenty thousand dollars someone spent on my stained dress is a drop in the ocean for him.

My foot is feeling much better now, but we've been traipsing around the island for a few hours and I'm enjoying the break, so I don't say anything.

"And if I can get through this first year of nonsense, I might actually get to do some accounting at some point."

"What nonsense?" he asks.

"My manager is a bit… overbearing," I say. "And I have to be her PA for a year before I can move into the actual accountancy department. So the first year doesn't even count toward accreditation."

Jonah looks up at me with a brow lifted. "So, she hires the best and brightest graduates she can find, just to make them sit around while she barks orders at them?" he asks. "Sounds like she has some issues to me."

He releases my foot and sits back against the tree behind him, leaning his head against it and closing his eyes.

"How's your head now?" I ask.

"So-so."

64

"So do you normally get blind drunk on your own? I ask. "Or was it a special occasion?"

There's a long pause that seems to stretch out forever in the quiet of the forest. I hear a couple of birds singing to each other, the big palm leaves swishing across each other in the light breeze, and then Jonah takes a deep, heavy breath, and sighs it out before speaking.

"Yesterday was the anniversary of my mom's death."

I feel like the entire world is getting smaller. Shrinking down to a tiny little glass globe that contains only Jonah and me, and this very important thing he's shared with me that brings up a sudden rush of my own emotions.

"I'm so sorry," I say, my voice cracking with emotion. "I shouldn't have asked. And definitely not like *that*."

"Don't sweat it," he says, his eyes still closed.

It takes every ounce of mental resistance I have not to close the gap between us and hug him, to let him know that I know this pain, and I understand, and I'm sorry.

"How long?" I ask.

"Nine years."

"Thirteen for me," I say.

That makes him open his eyes. He lifts his head and looks over at me.

"Thirteen years since your mom died?"

I nod. "Almost fourteen."

"How old were you?" he asks.

"Eleven."

His shoulder slump and he breathes out a deep sigh, shaking his head. "That's rough."

"Yeah," I say. "But so is losing your mom at... what? You would have been twenty-two?"

"Twenty-one," he clarifies. "But I was grown. You were just a kid."

I can't help but be a little endeared by the way he tries to minimize his pain now that he knows I carry my own.

"I doubt it's easy at any age," I say.

"True," he replies, and I can see from his expression that he's shared as much as he wants to for now. "You ready to roll? I think I saw Liam and Dale heading for the last clue just after we found it."

"Sure," I say. "Can't let them beat us."

Jonah ties the blindfold back around my head, and we set off again.

I guess he's feeling a bit better, or maybe the fact that we've shared a common wound with each other has made things a little easier between us, because instead of walking in silence as we have for most of the day, we end up chatting as we go.

"So how come you didn't ask Robbie for the money to do the internship?" he asks. "You two seem tight."

"I dunno," I say, trailing behind him. My steps are more certain now, as though a few hours of being led around by Jonah has made me more trusting of him.

"I guess... We're from a small town, both grew up without anything. And money can make things weird. Especially between family, which is what Robbie is to me. And honestly? Making it on my own is really important to me."

"I can respect that," he says.

"Well, you *are* a self-made billionaire," I say, chuckling.

"No," he says, firmly. "It's not the same."

That takes me by surprise. "What do you mean?"

"Don't get me wrong, we worked hard. Still do. And sure, it's impressive what we've achieved. But Matt and I are both from reasonably well-off families. We both had our moms into adulthood. We both went to good schools, great colleges, and our parents paid for it all. We secured the first investor for our company from a connection we made at an elite college. It's not the same. Unless your dad is secretly a millionaire and you're just LARPing as a plucky go-getter with the determination of an ox, it's not remotely the same."

I laugh, not quite sure whether to feel complimented or patronized.

"Well my dad's an alcoholic," I blurt.

Jonah doesn't respond. I can't see his face or read anything about his reaction, but talking about it after months of working in the city and making only superficial connections is cathartic, so I go on.

"Don't judge him, though," I say.

Still nothing.

"He was a great dad when I was a kid. We used to go on all sorts of adventures together. He just couldn't cope after my mom died. They were childhood sweethearts, you know? Together since they were fifteen, and my mom

67

didn't have me until she was forty. And then all of a sudden she was just gone, and the grief… it just crushed him."

I realize that Jonah has stopped walking, so I tilt my head up to roughly where I think he might be.

"Don't feel bad for me," I say. "Brenda noticed. She took me in and I spent most of my time in her house after that. I'm fine. Really. I shouldn't have said anything."

"You don't need to keep anything from me," he says, quietly. "I won't judge you, okay?"

In the darkness, I consider his words.

"Okay?" he repeats.

"Okay," I say. "But let's talk about something else?"

"If you want," says Jonah.

I feel his hand move on mine, turning until we're palm-to-palm, and he gently, slowly laces his fingers between mine and squeezes my hand. My tummy rolls over. I feel my pulse quicken a little at the feeling of his thick fingers between mine, gently clasping my hand in a way that is definitely closer to lovers than friendly-acquaintance scavenging buddies.

"Okay?" he says, and I'm not sure if he's asking whether it's okay for him to hold my hand like that or if it's okay to move on.

But it doesn't really matter, because the answer is the same on both counts. "Yes," I say, and he starts walking again.

We manage to find the seventh token first. The clue was "I'm filled up but I never go down. Dig deep and don't drown," and we figured it out pretty quickly. I can smell

68

the chlorine of the swimming pool when we arrive, even if I can't see it.

"There it is," says Jonah, pulling my blindfold off. "In the deep end, of course. One of us is going to have to dive for it."

"Not me," I say, still blinking. "I wore the blindfold. You do the diving."

Jonah looks at me with pursed lips, like he's actually thinking about arguing the point, but he gives up as soon as I lay my hand on my hip and raise an eyebrow at him.

"Fine," he says, pulling his shirt off over his head.

My gaze glues itself to the broad expanse of his chest. It's not the first time I've seen him topless, but it's the first time I've seen him topless up-close since my bikini malfunction. There's a smattering of curly little sand-colored hairs on his chest, and his pecs look toned and smooth. But also, somehow, soft. I have a sudden urge to reach out and poke one to find out, but Jonah puts an end to that particular train of thought as he shoves his t-shirt into my face.

"Hold this," he says and leans on a nearby table to kick his sneakers off.

Looking into the pool, I can clearly see four tokens at the bottom, shimmering, waiting to be claimed by each of the four teams. There doesn't seem to be anyone here to check up on us this time—I guess Matt figured that if we got this far, we wouldn't be likely to throw it all away by cheating.

"Is it heated?" I ask. "The pool?"

I look back to Jonah, who is leaning against a chair in nothing but his shorts, stretching his muscles like a statue of a Greek god, and I realize that I truly do not care whether the pool is heated or not. He takes a breath to answer me, but then his gaze shifts over my shoulder and his eyes widen. I spin around to see Liam rounding the corner, leading his blindfolded husband along behind him.

"Oh my God!" says Liam.

"What?" asks Dale.

"We could win! It's Fran and Jonah."

"No!" I shout. We've been ahead of everyone all day, but I guess the breaks and the chatting slowed us down enough to let them catch up.

I spin around with a look of horror on my face, but Jonah is already in mid-air, his arms stretched out above his head, diving into the pool.

I turn back to see Dale blinking and squinting, his blindfold now in his hand, while Liam hops toward the pool, pulling off his shoes with one hand and his vest with the other.

"Go, Jonah!" I shout.

There's a loud splash and Liam is in the pool as well, only a little behind Jonah.

"Come on, Liam!" shouts Dale, coming over to stand beside me. He gives me a friendly wink and links his arm into mine, but I can't keep my attention on him when there's so much at stake.

"Get the token!" I shout, as Liam and Jonah both dive towards the same spot, side-by-side.

"May the best man win!" says Dale.

"GET THE FUCKING TOKEN JONAH!" I scream.

Speak of the devil, and a moment later he bursts through the surface, his arm raised in triumph, fingers wrapped around the token.

"Yes!" I shout. "Come on come on let's go go go!"

"Put your blindfold on!" Jonah shouts, swimming toward the steps.

I start to smooth out the blindfold with my hands and glance over at Dale, but I don't have time to consider the curious smile he's got on his face. Jonah is back at my side with Liam barely two paces behind him. Screw neatness— I loop the crumpled blindfold around my head and plunge myself back into the darkness.

"Let's go," Jonah shouts, grabbing my hand and lacing his fingers tightly between mine.

I can hear the wet, sloppy sounds of his sodden feet against the stone path as I lurch along behind him, shoving his t-shirt into the waistband of my shorts.

Liam and Dale are somewhere close by, but I can't tell if they're behind us or ahead of us.

"What's happening?" I shout between heavy pants.

"Run faster!" says Jonah.

"I've only got little legs!"

"Keep going, babe!" I hear Liam shouting. Slightly ahead of us, maybe.

"Shit," hisses Jonah under his breath.

He stops suddenly, and before I know what's happening he's scooped me up with one hand under my legs and the other behind my back, just the way he rescued me from the lake almost exactly a year ago.

"Hold on!" he says, and I grab around his neck and cling to him, as tightly as I can.

He takes off—*fast*. Every time his foot lands on the floor I feel it reverberate through my whole body. His breath is loud. He takes great, heaving gulps of air and I can barely hear anything else. I have no idea where Liam and Dale are. But I can just make out the sound of cheering and whooping, and it's growing louder by the second. There must be a crowd of people waiting for us at the finish line. Which means we must be getting close—really close.

I hear a cry of "No!" to my right, but Jonah doesn't stop.

A few juddering steps later, I hear the air horn blow, and Matt's voice shouts, "Winner!"

Jonah puts me down immediately, and I rip my blindfold off, my heart slamming in my chest like an angry rhino. The afternoon sun attacks my eyes, and I blink and blink until things start to come into focus.

Jonah is bent over beside me, his hands on his knees, breathing in and out like a bellows. A little ways behind him, Dale is getting up off the floor, brushing sand from his knees, and apologizing to Liam, who is, in turn, telling Dale not to worry, and reassuring his husband that he still loves him.

I gasp as the realization sets in.

"We won?" I ask, looking up to Jonah as he rises to his full height.

He looks down at me with an expression on his face that I haven't seen before. He looks relaxed despite still being out of breath, and there's a shimmer in his eyes. He nods his head.

"Oh my God!" I shout, launching myself at him. Excitement and joy take over and I wrap my arms around his neck and my legs around his waist, screaming at the top of my lungs.

"Yeeees!" I punch the air, as the crowd claps and laughs at my reaction.

I catch Robbie's eye and she nods to me. She's the only one who really understands how much this means to me, and what I'm planning to do with my brand new Harley Davison motorcycle. Well, her and Jonah.

I lean down and smack a huge kiss onto Jonah's cheek.

"Thank you!" I grin at him. "Thank you, thank you, thank you. Best. Partner. Ever!"

I squeeze around his neck again, and I feel his thick, strong arms slide around my middle, squeezing me back.

"You're very welcome," he says quietly, still catching his breath. "And thank you. I'm going to enjoy my new bike."

I pull back and look at him. "It's not yours *yet*." I grin. "But I might let you take it for a spin around the island."

"Oh, is that right?" he smirks with a brow raised.

I nod at him, and that familiar tension crackles between us again. Almost as strong as it was when he brushed his thumb along my whiskey-soaked lips, except this time I'm wrapped around him and he's wearing me like a muffler.

I feel his arms squeeze a little tighter like he doesn't at all mind me being right where I am. I get the impression that he wouldn't mind if I stayed there forever, but I'm also a little jaded at this point. There's a nagging feeling at the back of my mind that's just waiting for the spell to break, and for Jonah to close himself off again.

"Well done, you two!"

Sure enough, Robbie's voice seems to do the trick, and Jonah's mask slips firmly back into place as he sets me down on the sand. *Welcome back, Friendly Acquaintance Jonah*, I think to myself ruefully. *I haven't missed you at all.* But there's no time to dwell. Robbie folds me into a big hug, and I hug her right back.

"Thanks," I say. "It was really fun, actually. I can't believe you set this whole thing up."

"It was mostly Matt," she laughs. "He's done loads of these on the island. He seems to like torturing people."

"Yeah, Jonah told me," I say. I turn around to look at him, but he's not there. In fact, he's not anywhere in our little crowd anymore.

"Well deserved," says Liam as he and Dale come over to join us. He holds his hand out to me, very sportsmanlike. I reach out and shake it.

"We'd have had you if I didn't trip over my own feet!" grins Dale, but he also holds out his hand to shake mine. "Congratulations!"

"Thanks," I reply, "but it's not like I was much help at the end. I was basically luggage."

Everyone laughs, and whatever hard feelings there may have been seem to disappear. I catch some movement in my peripheral vision and glance up towards the house, and my heart sinks a little when I see Jonah heading in through the side door. He didn't even hang around for a few minutes to bask in the glory of our win.

"Come on," says Liam. "Let's get some drinks."

"Great idea," says Robbie. "Mom and Anna have been drinking on the deck since about thirty minutes after you all set off."

"No way!" I exclaim.

"Way," she says. "Anna got a blister because she only brought new sneakers, Mom was "attacked"—her words—by a crab on the beach, and they both decided that they didn't really want a motorcycle after all."

"Sounds about right," I laugh. "What about Trish and Will?"

"They came to the library for the second clue, saw Mom and Anna out on the deck, and it was game over."

I shake my head, grinning. "Well, we can't let them all drink alone. Let's go!"

As we make our way back to the villa, Robbie links her arm in mine and leans in to whisper conspiratorially to me. "As one of the organizers, I'm not really supposed to say this. But I'm so glad you won, Fran."

"Me too," I sigh. "It's a huge weight off."

She unlinks her arm as we reach the deck. Matt is already there, having apparently had the same idea we did.

"Lucky you had such a motivated partner," she whispers with a smile, as she pulls away to join her husband.

Chapter 6

I didn't sleep well last night. I kept tossing and turning. Thinking about how much easier the rest of my internship will be with the money from selling the bike led me to thinking about Jonah, which led me to thinking about how unpredictable he is, which led me to thinking about how intimate our conversation in the forest was when he told me about his mom, which led me to thinking about my mom, which made me sad. Then I'd manage to clear my head, and my legs would start aching from all the walking yesterday, which would lead me to start thinking about us winning, and the whole vicious cycle would begin all over again.

I spent most of the day resting and reading on the beach behind the house, not wanting to encounter Jonah. I'm still pissed at his quick exit from the scavenger hunt celebrations yesterday. Plus, people have been arriving all day, getting settled into their rooms before the anniversary party tonight, and I was feeling too tired and grouchy to be sociable.

But the house has been quiet for the last couple of hours, apart from the occasional hum of a hairdryer or the kids running through the corridors. Everyone's busy getting ready for the party, which is supposed to kick off at seven. I'm standing in my room at seven thirty, slicking on some lip gloss and mascara, when there's a knock at the door.

"Yeah?" I call.

"Hey," says Robbie through the door. "Can I come in?"

"Sure," I call back.

She pushes open the door, closes it behind her, and shoots me a quick smile as she walks over to sit on the bed. "Everything OK?" she asks. "Or are you just being fashionably late?"

"I'm great," I tell her. "I just fell asleep for a bit when I got out of the shower. It's the first time since yesterday that my legs have stopped aching."

"God," she says. "I almost did the same, and I wasn't even scavenging yesterday. Has it sunk in yet that you actually won?"

"Yes," I grin, picking up my earrings and leaning into the mirror to thread them through my ears. "It'll be such a huge help."

Robbie doesn't say anything. For a while, after she started making money through her royalties, she'd take opportunities like this to offer to help me out. And even though she's always been the more stubborn of us ever since we were kids, she finally got the message that on this particular issue, I would not budge.

"So everyone got here on time?"

"Yeah," says Robbie. "No surprise flight delays or sunken yachts."

I laugh a little and shake my head. "Can't say I've been to many parties where guests canceling because their yacht sunk was a real concern," I say. "It'll be a fun night."

I'm not sure how much I believe this. I adore being here with Robbie, Matt, Brenda, Anna, Will, and Trish. Even Jonah, when he's not being distant. But seeing all the yachts and seaplanes lining up around the island has given me a nagging insecurity in the pit of my stomach like I don't belong among all these super successful people. Imposter syndrome, I guess you'd call it, but knowing what it's called hasn't helped get rid of it. And sure, there are plenty of guests who are from the same place as me and are not super-wealthy billionaires, and I probably shouldn't care either way, but I can't really control the fact that I do. I wish I could be more like Anna, who would gladly walk into a boardroom full of Fortune 500 CEOs and give them all the finger if she thought they deserved it.

I plan to find a corner to sit in, and just avoid the people I don't know—and Jonah, since I can't handle much more of his nonsense. I'm not playing his hot-and-cold game anymore. He's like Russian Roulette—it starts off exciting, sure, but the end is no fun at all.

Robbie hasn't said anything. When I look in the mirror, I find her staring at me with her head slightly tilted.

"What?" I ask.

"Hmm?" she says, innocently.

"I can tell you want to ask me something. Spit it out."

Robbie rolls her eyes, but she can't deny the truth.

"Oh, nothing," she says. "I just noticed that you and Jonah seem to be spending a bit of time together, that's all."

"What, at the scavenger hunt? You put us on a team together!" I accuse.

"Well, yes," she agrees. "But you were with him in the bar the night before."

"I was exploring and he was already in there."

"And Mom said you looked pretty cozy the day you arrived."

"I lost my bikini top!" I say, my voice getting higher. "Because he ran right into me and then fireman-carried me all the way down the beach."

"Mmmmhmmm," says Robbie, wearing a smile I don't like one bit. "And at the wedding, you two disappeared together."

"Because. I. Fell. In. The. Lake." I say.

"Right," she says, nodding. "Of course. I was just wondering because I remember the first time you met him when you flirted outrageously with each other and you told me you'd slide down him like a fire station pole."

I can feel my cheeks reddening. "That was… I…" I pause and frown at her. "That was when he was just a random stranger and I didn't know I'd end up kinda-in-laws with him."

"Okay," she says, annoyingly.

We fall into silence for a minute, but I can't leave it there.

"Look, he's hot," I say. "And I like him. And would I have a fling with him on his private island in the middle of Paradise? Of course."

"Of course," echoes Robbie.

"But he flirts, I flirt back, he goes cold and pulls away and avoids me until the next time, and—" I shoot her a reproachful look. "God *damn* it, how have you gotten me to talk about this?!"

Robbie laughs. "I'm your best friend. It's my job."

"I hate you," I say.

"You love me," she says, casually. "And don't let it get to you if he's being like that. Matt says he hasn't had a proper relationship since college."

Part of me is surprised that he's had a proper relationship at all. I've seen pictures of him in magazines, attending this fundraiser or that premiere with a model on his arm, and I figure he just keeps it simple and whores his way through a long line of willing, beautiful women.

"There will be plenty of eligible bachelors here tonight anyway," says Robbie, getting up from the bed. "Just saying."

I roll my eyes at her. "Well, I'm just going to drink spritzers with your mom," I say.

"Maybe you can get matching old lady shawls," Robbie teases, and I pick up the cushion from the accent chair beside me and throw it at her.

"Get out!'

"I'm going, I'm going," she says. "Love you."

"Shut up," I say, smiling at her. "Oh hey, Robbie?"

She stops on her way to the door and looks back.

"Happy anniversary," I say. "Best couple I know."

"Thanks," she says, with a genuine smile on her face. "Now hurry up, everyone's asking where you are."

≈

The party is in full swing by the time I arrive. I'm amazed at the job the staff have done in only a few hours. The deck area in front of the house has been completely transformed—there are small paper lanterns on strings hanging between every wooden pole and pillar, tropical flower arrangements adorn every seat and table, and lit flashlights are running all the way down the path and onto the beach, where a wooden tiki bar has been set up.

I don't recognize most of the people who've arrived during the day. Everyone looks very summer casual, and there are an inordinate number of men in Hawaiian shirts standing around chatting very seriously over multicolored cocktails with tiny umbrellas in them.

One man who's just about ten feet away from me drains his drink and looks in my direction. When he locks eyes with me, I smile. He's pretty good-looking. Not as good-looking as Jonah, but few men are. This guy has dark hair, dark eyes, and an impeccably manicured goatee.

When I smile, he starts toward me. I feel a knot in my stomach immediately. Not the sort of knot I have when Jonah decides to blow hot instead of cold, but a knot of social anxiety, and that pesky imposter syndrome I've been feeling all day. I haven't even had a single drink to temper it yet.

I think back to Robbie's words and try to calm myself as the goatee guy gets closer. I love her, and I trust her. And if she thinks that the eligible bachelors at this party might be good for me, then I'll take her word for it.

I feel a little ripple of confidence and square my shoulder slightly, locking eyes with the approaching man again. I pretty up my smile a bit more and draw in a breath, about to say hi.

"Thanks," he says flatly, holding out his empty glass and a plate with a couple of crumbs on it.

I reach for them automatically, and it doesn't really register that I've been mistaken for staff until he walks away, leaving me holding his empties.

Now, I don't mind being taken for staff on a normal day. I was a server for years and I have a great deal of respect for the people who are working this party tonight. They're the ones who make this place a paradise, and quietly keep it running so their bosses don't have to think about a thing.

But I'm wearing my best dress, damn it. A bright yellow maxi number that contrasts with my freshly tanned skin and makes my dark hair and eyes pop.

Before the irritation even has a chance to set in, two big hands come into view, one plucking the plate from me, and the other taking the glass. I look up into Jonah's chiseled face, but he's looking off in the direction that Goatee Guy went, frowning.

"Hey," I say.

He looks down at me, but he doesn't speak immediately. His eyes trail down my dress, then back up past the curls on my shoulder to my eyes. I feel like I've been *inspected* by him, and much to my own chagrin I don't dislike it.

"Hello, Franchesca," he says.

"Fran," I say. He ignores me, studying my face for a moment.

"Why are you annoyed?" he asks.

I consider saying that I'm not, or that it doesn't matter, but something about the sincerity in his expression makes me blurt it out.

"Because I was already feeling way out of my depth, and then that douchebag," I nod in Goatee Guy's general direction, lowering my voice so I'm not overheard, "mistook me for a server. In my best dress!"

Jonah glances over towards Goatee Guy again, then looks down at my dress, and back up to my face.

A member of staff—a real one—passes by, and Jonah calls her over. He puts the plate and glass down on the tray she's carrying, plucks a couple of glasses full of bubbly from it, and then looks her in the eye and smiles.

"Thank you, Tracy," he says, nodding to her in gratitude.

When she's gone, Jonah passes me one of the glasses.

"Why do you feel out of your depth?" he asks. I wasn't expecting this to be an inquisition, but something about how straightforwardly he asks the question compels me to answer.

"Because," I say, "Everyone here is super successful and I'm just an intern with—"

"Don't do that," Jonah cuts in.

I stare up at him.

"Don't downplay your own achievements." He looks deadly serious. "You've worked hard to get where you are and you're only just beginning your career. You're smart. And kind. And capable. Don't devalue any of that."

I keep staring in silence, my brows raised in surprise.

"That guy is Edward Philmore," he says, nodding in the direction of Goatee Guy. The party is pretty loud by now, and Jonah keeps his voice low enough that only I can hear it.

"He's a hanger-on. Nobody likes him, specifically because of how he treats people. He's only here because he happened to be lurking around his brother, Beckett, when he was invited, and Matt felt it would be rude not to invite Edward too."

I let my gaze trail over to Philmore, who is sipping on a new glass of bubbly from Tracy's tray—drinking alone, I note, much like he was when I first spotted him.

"They're from a well-off family," Jonah goes on. "Beckett started his own business and he's doing really well. He couldn't be here tonight because he's in Oz on business. But Eddie just hangs around, sucking up to his father and waiting to inherit his business so he can piss it down the drain."

I purse my lips and look up at Jonah. He raises his brows at me.

"Well?" he says. "How out of your depth do you feel now? I mean, if you want to feel inferior to a guy who's literally never done anything in his life, Franchesca, be my g—"

"Fran."

He cracks a slight smile. "But it just doesn't make any sense."

He's got me there. But I'm still a bit flummoxed by how highly Jonah seems to regard me and my achievements. I just assumed that to him, at his level of success, I'd be an ant.

"Fine," I say. "Well, point me in the direction of an eligible bachelor who's not a douchebag."

His attention snaps back to me, and there's something dark in his expression.

"One that won't cut and run every time I flirt with them," I say, a bit surprised at my own boldness.

He stares at me with his eyes slightly narrowed, and his breaths seem to be coming a little faster than before. But I stare right back at him, daring him to deny it.

"Fran!"

We snap out of our staring contest as Eric—Matt's driver, who I know from Meadow Hill when he came to help out at Will's Café a couple of years ago—comes bounding over towards us, a big smile on his face.

"Eric!" I say, returning his smile. "Robbie didn't tell me you were going to be here."

"Well, here I am." He says, his grin widening. He nods to Jonah. "Hey."

"Hey," says Jonah, flatly. His mind is pretty clearly elsewhere.

"Is Fiona here, as well? And Clara?" I ask.

"My lovely wife is indeed here… somewhere," says Eric. "We left Clara at my sister's place, she'd already arranged to take her on a camping trip with her cousins."

"Excuse me," says Jonah, suddenly. He nods to each of us in turn and takes off through the throng of people.

I watch him go for a second, mentally rolling my eyes, and turn back to Eric. "Sounds like fun," I say. "Though I think you and Fiona might have the better end of the deal."

"Yeah," he nods. "It's a beautiful place, right? I keep telling Matt to build a road so I can drive him around whenever he comes here, but no luck. I'll have to make do with waiting for invites to the parties."

I laugh, and we chat a little more, catching up on what's been going on since the last time we saw each other. Eric eventually excuses himself to go and find his wife.

I consider finding someone I know to sit with, but then I think about what Jonah said, and decide that I'll mingle a little instead. I'm sure half these people do business in New York, so if nothing else it might be a good networking opportunity for the future.

Considering my earlier trepidation, I'm surprised by how easily I manage to speak with everyone I approach, or who approaches me. It's just general chit-chat, and whenever anyone asks what I do I just say "accounting" instead of going into specifics. Nobody, it seems, is interested in knowing any more than that.

I speak with CEOs, entrepreneurs, lawyers, doctors, and even a stunt man who went to college with Matt and Jonah and claims to have worked on some movie with Chris Hemsworth, though he won't give me any juicy details.

At one point, as a particularly chatty woman excuses herself from my company, I look up and see Jonah on the other side of the deck, looking right at me. He dips his head to me as though to say "told you so," and I smile and shake my head, lifting my glass to him.

Late in the night, when more than a few words are being slightly slurred and I haven't overheard a conversation about a business deal in over an hour, one of the house staff bangs a gong to gather everyone down on the beach.

"Ladies and Gentlemen," calls Jonah, once everyone has assembled. A hush descends on the crowd.

"We are here tonight to celebrate the first anniversary of the marriage of my best friend and business partner, the esteemed Matthew Sullivan." A ripple of applause goes through the crowd, and Matt, who has his arm around Robbie, nods to Jonah.

"And his far more attractive, far too good for him, much more famous and universally adored wife, Roberta Sullivan."

"Oh, stop," says Robbie, and everyone chuckles.

"Now, as we all know, having been at the wedding, theirs was a fairytale beginning."

"Aye, aye!" calls a drunk man from the tiki bar.

"Thank you, Frederick," says Jonah, deadpan, to more laughter.

"But we also know that marriage isn't about the first day, so much as every day that comes after."

There's a murmur of agreement, and I notice Eric from the corner of my eye, pulling Fiona close to him and wrapping his arm around her shoulders.

"It's about finding that one person who you can be with every waking moment without ever getting bored," he says, and when I look back at him, he's looking right at me through the crowd. My heart misses a beat.

"It's about having the courage to find the person who will bind their soul with yours, who'll carry your joys and your pain along with you, who will love you through your worst moments and celebrate your best…"

"Aww," says someone a little to my right. I don't know who, because I can't tear my eyes away from Jonah, who is still staring at me. Staring at me so intently that a woman in front of me turns around and looks at me. A jolt of panic surges through me—if she's noticed, then other people might have too.

"…and to say to the world, 'this person is mine'," Jonah goes on. "And I will always be theirs, through everything."

Jonah finally looks away from me, over to where Matt is pulling Robbie closer and pressing a kiss to the top of her head.

"And I think anyone who knows these two will tell you that theirs is one of the rarest matches made in heaven."

Jonah raises his glass. "So here's to love," he says. "And to Matt and Robbie."

"Matt and Robbie!" calls everyone in unison.

When the toast dies down, Jonah speaks again.

"Now, I have no idea what sort of gift you give to the couple who has everything, but here's a little token of my appreciation for you two."

He turns around and lifts his arm into the air, and a high-pitched squeal echoes across the beach as a firework shoots into the air and explodes into a dozen red blooms of light, arranged in the shape of a heart.

Everyone oohs and aahs as more fireworks whistle their way into the cloudless sky and explode into a beautiful array of colors.

I glance back down, but Jonah's gone. Everyone around me seems to be huddled into a couple, looking up at the sky. Even the stuntman has paired off with the chatty lady from earlier. I wrap my arms around myself, not quite sure what I'm feeling after Jonah's speech.

It seemed so heartfelt. Maybe that's why he gets weird about flirting. Maybe he's a true romantic looking for all the things he mentioned, and since he knows I'm not *the one*, he doesn't want to get too attached to me. Although I have a hard time reconciling the man who gave that speech with the one I've seen in magazine spreads, models dangling from either arm.

"Here she is!"

Anna and Brenda are suddenly right there on either side of me. Brenda opens up her old lady shawl and slips one side of it over my shoulders, pulling me into a side-hug.

"Beautiful, isn't it?" she asks, winking at me.

"Yeah," I reply, grateful to be saved from thinking far too much about something that will be completely irrelevant to my life in a few days' time when I'm back in New York. I look up into the sky and let the fireworks melt my worries away. "Yeah, it really is."

Chapter 7

The next couple of days pass in a pleasant, hazy blur of swimming and reading and relaxing, walking on the beach with Robbie, and enjoying al fresco dinners in the evening. Everyone who arrived for the party left the next day, before noon, so it's just been family and friends since then. Which suits me just fine. I've barely seen Jonah, who seems to have taken to avoiding me since the party, which is also fine by me. Better that than his weird moods, even if I'm starting to think that it might make things a little bit difficult during the flight home. But there's very little drama or intrigue happening in paradise these days —and once again, this suits me juuuuust fine.

Until the evening of the third day, that is. In the after-dinner lull, I go to the reading room to return a book I borrowed. I touch my hand to the door handle, but before I can open it I hear voices from inside and freeze.

"You have to let it go, man." It's Matt's voice. "It was nine years ago."

"To the day," says Jonah, who sounds like he's slurring his words a bit.

I guess they're talking about his mom, but "let it go" seems like an odd thing to say.

"Look, I know it hurt you," says Matt. "But if you keep holding onto it, it's just gonna keep dragging you down."

"I'm fine," I hear Jonah say flatly.

"You're not fine," says Matt, sounding exasperated. "And we both know why it's hitting you so much harder than usual. You *have* to let it go."

I decide that I've heard enough. Whatever is going on in there is not for me, and I feel uncomfortable sticking around and eavesdropping on it. I can return my book later.

I head back to my room to start packing up some of my things since we'll be leaving the day after tomorrow. I figure since the vacation's almost over I should check my phone, which I have been very consciously ignoring since arriving here, to see what's going to be waiting for me when I get back. I pick it up, and my heart jumps in my chest a little—I have eight missed calls from Sarah. The little notification bubble on my email app is showing "99+" as well.

I briefly consider ignoring Sarah's calls. If I had a secure, full-time job, I probably would, but principles are not a luxury interns can afford. With a sigh, I hit the "call back" button, and Sarah picks up almost at once.

"Oh, thank God," she says. "Where are you?"

"I'm… on vacation?" I say.

"Right," says Sarah. "Of course you are."

"Sooo…" I trail off, giving her the chance to tell me it can wait until next week.

"So Jessica saw a picture of you," she says. "On Instagram."

"Okay," I say, quickly wracking my brains for any ridiculous or compromising pictures that might be lurking online from my youth.

"You were with a bunch of CEOs. Roberta Sullivan was there as well."

"Aha," I say, relaxing a little. I was the model of moderation at the party, so at least it's not a photo of me drunkenly cavorting. "Yeah. That was a couple of days ago."

"Yeah," says Sarah. "Well, Jessica told me to call you and tell you to do some networking for the company. Y'know, try to get us a few new clients."

I open my mouth, but nothing comes out at first. The sheer audacity of it has taken me by surprise.

"Does she have any idea what boundaries are?" I ask.

Sarah snorts on the other end of the line. "You know she doesn't," she says.

I sigh.

"Well, I can't now, even if I wanted to—which, for the record, I don't. Everyone's gone home. They were just here for the party."

"Roberta Sullivan's anniversary party, right?" asks Sarah, dreamily. It's so strange to hear her constantly full-name Robbie like that. Especially with her married name.

"Right," I say.

"She mentioned that she's been trying to get a meeting with Sullivan Wells for ages."

"Oh God," I groan. "Did you tell her I'm Robbie's friend?"

"Is that what you call her?" asks Sarah excitedly. "Such a cool name."

"Sarah, focus."

"No, I didn't tell her. When do I ever get a chance to actually say anything to her?" she asks, which is a fair point.

"Okay," I say, relieved. There are many things I'll do to get ahead in this internship, but using my friends isn't one of them. "Well, don't. Just tell her I was invited by a friend of a friend."

"Will do," says Sarah. "Are you having a good time? Jessica showed me the pictures. You looked amazing in that dress."

"Thanks," I say. "Yeah, I'm having a good time. It's beautiful here. You should see the—"

"Oh. Shit. She's back," Sarah whispers urgently, and the line goes dead.

I sit there for a minute, marveling at how one woman can put everyone around her so on edge. I'm sure it's not good for productivity, and it's certainly not what I aspire to, but it's still impressive in its own way.

I slip my phone back onto the nightstand and survey the room. I have an uncanny ability to absolutely trash any space I'm in for more than a few minutes, completely unintentionally, so it takes me a good hour to gather and pack away all my clothes, makeup, jewelry, and other bits and pieces. I leave the clothing I'm wearing tomorrow on top, along with—reluctantly—warmer clothes to put on before we reach New York.

When I'm done, the only thing that remains out of place is the book on the end of my bed—the one I tried to return earlier. I pick it up and head back toward the reading room, assuming it'll be free by now. I grab my water bottle as well so I can fill it on my way back.

I pause at the door of the reading room and listen, just in case anyone's still inside. Everything is quiet, so I turn the handle and push the door open.

I only get half a step into the room before I realize it's not actually empty. I freeze, staring across the room at Jonah's huge form, slumped in an armchair.

It takes me a moment to see that he's asleep. There's a bottle of whiskey beside him and a glass in his hand, resting precariously on his leg, undoubtedly destined to tumble to the floor if he shifts in his sleep.

I slip my book quietly back onto the shelf, and look over at Jonah, wondering whether I should intervene.

He looks so peaceful. I mean, the room stinks of whiskey, but his face is so placid, completely devoid of the little frowns that often plague it. His hair is scruffed up at the back like he's been sleeping for a while. I don't want to wake him, but I also don't want the staff to have to spend the evening getting whiskey out of the carpet.

As quietly and gently as I can, I slide the glass out from between his fingers and place it down on the table beside the bottle. There's a light blanket on the footstool beside the chair, so I shake it out and lay it over him. He stirs slightly as it settles on him.

"Shhh," I whisper. "It's okay. Go back to sleep."

One of his eyes opens lazily and focuses on me. A smile lifts one side of his mouth, but he's in no fit state to wake up and start chatting. The eye closes again, but a hint of the smile remains on his sleeping face, and that's how I leave him.

"Hey, Fran."

Matt comes into the kitchen to grab a beer as I'm filling my water bottle. Everyone else is out on the deck, relaxing, enjoying their last night in paradise. Of course, they're going to be on a luxury yacht cruise for the next few weeks while I get to head back to my shoebox apartment and overbearing boss, so I don't feel *too* sorry for them.

"Hey," I shoot back. "Are you all ready to set off tomorrow?"

"Yup," he says. "Just about. It's a pity you can't come with us. I know Robbie really wanted you to."

"The trials of a lowly intern," I say, with mock resignation that isn't really all that mock.

"Cheers to the interns," he says, raising his bottle in my direction. "You coming outside?"

"Sure," I say, screwing the lid on my bottle.

Matt turns for the door, but I feel an impulse spark in my belly, and it erupts from my mouth before I can stop it.

"Hey, Matt?"

"Mmm?" he says, turning around.

"Can I ask you something and have you not be mad at me for asking?"

"Uh," he says, looking confused. He places his beer down on the kitchen island and gives me his full attention. "Sure."

I press my lips together, trying to think of a tactful way to ask what I want to ask. But then I realize there's no such thing.

"Does Jonah have a drinking problem?"

Matt snorts. "No!" he says, shaking his head. But then he pauses and sighs. "I guess you've noticed he's been wallowing a bit lately?"

"Yeah," I say, and then after a little hesitation, "He told me it was the anniversary of his mom's passing the other day."

"Yeah," says Matt. "And…"

Matt pauses for a moment, clearly debating whether to continue, and then thinks better of it.

"Something else," he says. "But it's not my place to tell anyone. I hope you understand."

I try to imagine myself in a similar situation, with someone asking me about Robbie's faults and most intimate secrets, and I realize that not even being dragged over vinegar-soaked glass would get me to spill.

"Of course," I say, with a genuine smile. "But… he's okay?"

"He will be," says Matt. "But I promise you he's not a drunk. He's the most stand-up guy I know."

"Okay," I say. "Thanks."

Matt smiles, picking up his beer again. "Shall we?"

"Sure," I say, and follow him out to the deck.

Chapter 8

I spend the whole of the next day with Robbie, basically stuck to her hip. I won't see her again for God knows how long, and I want to make the most of the time we have left. We spend a few hours down on the beach, go swimming a few times, and the rest of it on the deck, hanging out with whoever stops by.

The staff are busy all day, packing away equipment and ferrying luggage from the house to the boat. I barely see Jonah the whole day, but he makes sure to come down to the pier to see everyone off when the time comes for the yacht to set sail.

"Love you," says Robbie, giving me a tight squeeze.

"Love you, too," I say.

One by one, everyone gives me a hug and tells me they wish I were going with them. Brenda is watery-eyed and sniffling as she tells me to look after myself and make sure I eat enough, as though there's any chance of that not happening.

"I will," I promise her. "I'll try and get home for a visit soon. Thank you for looking after Dad."

"Don't you worry about that at all, love," she says. "You just focus on you and what you've got to do."

I pull her into a tight hug and squeeze. To my right, I overhear Matt talking quietly to Jonah.

"Think about what I said," he says. "We'll be back in a few weeks. You good?"

"I'm good," replies Jonah. They bear hug, and then everyone but Jonah and I traipses up the walkway to board the yacht.

It's a very long goodbye. They start waving as the yacht separates from the pier, but after a minute I realize that it's moving pretty slowly, actually. And my arm aches. So I stand beside Jonah with my arms wrapped around my torso and watch the boat get smaller and smaller, and wave again just before it disappears around the far end of the island.

"You didn't fancy a longer vacation?" I ask Jonah, once the boat is finally out of sight. He's standing just behind me, arms folded across his chest.

"I'm closing a deal next week," he says. "I need to be in Manhattan."

"Oh," I say.

I almost blurt that I work there—which he already knows —and suggest that we meet for a coffee. But there's no way a busy billionaire who's sometimes flirty with me on the rare occasions that we encounter each other because we're vaguely linked through our respective friends' marriage wants to meet up with me just because he's in town. And besides, I'd hate him to think I'm suggesting a date. He'd probably keel over.

"Okay. So what time should I be ready to leave tomorrow?" I ask.

"I figure we'll head out at about five?" he says.

"That late?" I ask, surprised.

"I have a remote meeting tonight with someone in Hong Kong," he says. "It doesn't start until 3 am and it'll likely run a few hours. I'll probably be asleep for most of the day."

"Oh," I say. "Okay. I guess I'll just have to spend the day in the pool, sunning myself. It's a hard life."

Jonah smirks, his arms still crossed over his chest.

"Well, the staff are all gone with Matt's group," he says. "So you'll have to get your own food and drinks. They'll have left some stuff in the residents' kitchen."

I press my hand to my chest in feigned shock. "But how will I, a lofty intern, ever manage to lower myself to the paltry task of preparing my own food?"

"I'm sure you'll manage," he says dryly.

"And here I was, thinking you'd offer to wait on me hand and foot."

He lifts a brow at me, and I grin back at him.

We head back to the kitchen together. Jonah grabs a bottle of water from the fridge and I refill mine from the tap.

"I need to do some prep work for my meeting, and try to get a nap in before it," he says. "Otherwise I'll be a zombie by the second hour."

"Right," I grin. "See you later."

"Later," he says.

He leaves the kitchen in the direction of his bedroom but pops his head back through the door a moment later.

"Franchesca?" he says.

At this point, I've just given up on trying to get him to call me Fran.

"Mm?"

"Thanks for the blanket," he says. He gives me a brief smile and disappears again.

For some reason, a warm feeling starts seeping through me when he says it. I try to tell myself to knock it off, but I don't seem to be listening.

~

Since Jonah's going to be busy and we're not leaving until tomorrow evening, I figure I'll have time to finish one more book before I go home. I barely get any time to read when I'm working, so I'll take what I can get.

I'm starting to get a bit stiff after a few hours of reading on the deck, so I head back to my room, change into my bikini, grab a towel, and head for the pool. I'm not planning on going for a swim, but I figure the sauna might loosen my muscles up a bit.

When I arrive, Jonah's already there, swimming lengths in the pool. I can hear the splash as he dives into the water before I see him, and I slow down, not wanting to intrude. The natural light is starting to fade a little, and his body is streaked with shimmering reflections from the water.

I stay at the corner, tucked into it, and watch him through the glass wall.

He really is magnificent. He glides through the water like a dolphin, his powerful arms slicing through the surface with barely a ripple. When he reaches the end of the pool, he dips into the water and under himself, then kicks off with his arms outstretched and glides almost half the length of the pool under the surface before he starts stroking again. Every four strokes, he draws in a breath.

It's almost a kind of meditation, watching him. The predictability of the movements mesmerizes me, the slow rhythm lulls me… and of course, the fact that he's insanely handsome doesn't hurt.

I watch the muscles on his back bunch as he heaves himself out of the pool, and yet somehow my brain doesn't register that he's finished swimming until he looks right at me.

"I'd have sold tickets if I knew there'd be spectators," he says.

I feel a flush rising on my cheeks, and I step out from behind the corner so as not to look like a total weirdo.

"Sorry," I say. "I just got here and I didn't want t—"

"Liar," he says.

"What?"

"You've been there ten minutes."

He's not wrong, but it's mortifying that he was aware I was watching him the whole time.

"Well I didn't want to disturb you," I say, defensively.

"You didn't," says Jonah, toweling himself off.

"Well… good!" I say, not knowing what else *to* say.

"Did you want to use the pool?" he asks, but it takes a couple of seconds for his question to register because I'm distracted by the rivulets of water dripping down his honey-toned skin, and the way his torso twists and stretches when he reaches up to run the towel over his hair.

"Uh," I say after a delay. "No. I was going to sit in the sauna for a bit."

Jonah wraps the towel around his waist and reaches inside it, and a second later his wet swim shorts make a loud *splat* on the floor.

"God!" I say, spinning around to look away from him.

"What?" he asks, a definite tone of amusement in his voice.

"You're naked!" I splutter. "You can't just strip like that in front of people."

"I'm not naked, I'm wearing a towel. I just don't want to drip all through the house."

"Right," I say. It's a perfectly reasonable explanation, but the fact that he's got nothing on under that towel has somehow flustered me. Annoyingly so.

"Hungry?" he asks.

"What?"

"Are you hungry?"

"For food?" I ask, without thinking. I can immediately feel a flush breaking out across my chest when I realize what I just said, and I have to fight to stop my body from curling up in a tight cringe. Jonah doesn't help me at all by

102

remaining completely silent for what seems like an eternity before he finally responds.

"That's an odd way to answer that question," he says, evenly.

"Nothing!" I blurt out before he's even finished speaking. "I'm a bit hungry, yes."

"You like steak?"

"Yes," I say, turning around to face him again.

"Good," he says, picking up his stuff from the table beside him. There's a laptop, a tablet, a phone, and a thick folder full of paper. I guess he's been doing his meeting prep here. "Is an hour long enough for your sauna?"

"Uh… sure."

"Alright," he says. "Dinner in an hour. See you then."

I stand there for a while, staring at the door he left through, wondering if he stashed a secret chef somewhere. For some reason, I just can't imagine him cooking a meal from scratch. I mean, he did help Matt with some grilling a few days ago, but that's not quite the same.

An hour later, after I've cooled down from my sauna and taken a shower, I find myself riffling through my packed luggage to find a dress for dinner. It's definitely not a date, but it still feels rude to show up in shorts and a vest when he's offered to cook for me. I settle on a white sun dress that comes to my knees, which is dotted here and there with little red flowers. I even slick on a little red-tinted lip gloss and some subtly smokey eye makeup.

Not for Jonah, I tell myself. But because my social life has been dry as a bone for the last 18 months, and I don't get many opportunities to dress up. I slide my feet into some white, strappy sandals with four-inch heels, and head down the long hall toward the kitchen.

The lights are dimmed when I walk in. The entire side of the room has been opened to the deck, and Jonah's set a small table out there for two, complete with a flickering candle in the middle, and a small vase with a single tropical flower in it. I haven't seen those particular flowers near the house—he must've walked halfway down the beach to pick it.

"How do you like it cooked?" comes a deep voice to my right.

"Jesus!" I say, jumping half out of my skin as I spin around. Jonah is standing there with a pair of cooking tongs in one hand and a wooden board in the other, upon which are two deep red steaks.

"There's literally nobody else around for hundreds of miles of ocean," he says, dryly. "Don't be so dramatic."

"Don't tell me what to be," I snipe back. I'm aware that my mood has fallen a bit since everyone I call family left the island, and the realization set in that I wouldn't see them again for a long time. That, and the fact that I'll be back under Jessica's boot in a few days.

"How do you like your steak cooked," he repeats, ignoring my little outburst.

"Medium well," I reply, a little sulkily.

"I'll do it medium rare," he says, and picks the steaks up one by one, dropping them both onto a sizzling hot pan.

"I said medium well!" I protest.

He gestures towards the sizzling steaks as he looks at me, an apologetic expression on his face. "Can't hear you!" he says, much too loudly, as though he's trying to shout across a construction yard.

The sizzling is loud, but it's not *that* loud. I press my lips together and frown at him, and he gives me a knockout grin that lights up his face and sends a jolt from my heart to my panties. He's *very* annoying when he's happy, but it's much better than seeing him sad and struggling.

"Have a seat," he calls. "It'll just be a few minutes."

I head out onto the deck and sit at the table, looking out across the ocean and enjoying the balmy evening breeze on my skin. Jonah puts on some music—jazz again, but this tune is much less melancholy than the one he was listening to in the bar the other night. It has a peppy beat to it, and I find myself tapping my foot as I wait.

"Okay," says Jonah, a few minutes later. "One medium rare steak with dauphinoise and asparagus tips."

He places the plate down in front of me, and my brows shoot up in surprise. The steak looks amazing, covered in a thin crust of dark brown caramelization. The asparagus is wrapped with some very thin slivers of ham and tied with what looks like the length of a single layer of scallion. And the dauphinoise is in its own little baking dish, still bubbling slightly around the edges and golden-brown on top.

"Wow," I say.

"What?" he asks. "You didn't think I could cook?"

"No, actually," I say. "I mean, why would you? You can afford a private chef."

"And I have one," he says.

"But once upon a time I was a student sharing a frat house with a band of savages, and I got sick of Hot Pockets and mac and cheese."

"Way to diss my entire diet," I say, and he grins. "Well, I'm very impressed."

"Wine?"

He lifts the carafe from the table and hovers it over my glass.

"Sure," I say. "Why not? It's the last day of my vacation."

He swirls the wine in the carafe and pours me a glass, then sets it down and pours himself some iced water.

"No wine for you?" I ask.

"I'm working later, remember?" he says.

It's not that I didn't believe Matt, exactly, when he told me that Jonah didn't have a drinking problem. But I did have a nagging doubt somewhere in the back of my mind that if someone asked *me* that question about *my* best friend, I would protect them even if it were true. So I find myself a little relieved to find that Jonah isn't just drowning himself in hard liquor every night. That he doesn't *have* to take a drink.

"Right," I say. "Oh, well. Cheers!"

We clink glasses and sip. I cut a corner off my steak and stare at it skeptically. It's far pinker than I would normally eat.

"How long have you been eating your steak medium well?" he asks.

"Since I've been eating steaks," I say.

"Trust me," he says. "Just try it. Close your eyes and see how you like it."

I raise one eyebrow at him over the top of my fork.

"Remember the whiskey?" he says. "You liked that, right?"

"Yes," I reply. I don't mention that I'm not actually sure whether I enjoyed the whiskey so much as I enjoyed the feeling of his fingers in my hair and the way he pressed the glass to my lips, but the mention of it takes me right back to that moment, and I can feel my cheeks turning hot.

"Well then," he says. "Go on."

I close my eyes and pop the steak into my mouth, and it immediately floods with a burst of delicious, savory juices.

"Mmm!" I say, my eyes flaring open.

Jonah is wearing his smug grin, but I don't care in the least. The steak tastes amazing. I'm almost sad for all the steaks that came before and how they're fading in comparison.

"Okay," I say when I've swallowed my mouthful. "I concede. It's good."

Jonah smiles with satisfaction, cutting into his own steak. His is even pinker than mine. Closer to red. I'm not sure I could eat it that way, and it makes me realize that it isn't that he thinks his way is the best for everyone—he *knew* that medium rare would be just right for me. Or maybe I'm reading too much into it. The wine is delicious and I took two big mouthfuls on an empty stomach, so I'll blame my overthinking on that.

I dig my fork into the dauphinoise and blow on it before putting it in my mouth. As soon as it hits my tongue, I am immediately transported back to Meadow Hill, to a cold winter's night at Robbie's house, sitting around the table with her, Brenda, and Anna and feeling safe.

"Oh my God," I say, looking over to Jonah. "I've had this before. This exact thing. It's B—"

"Brenda's recipe," he says, nodding. He's obviously delighted with my reaction. "She made it when I was at Robbie and Matt's house one night. You know how she loves to feed people…"

"She sure does," I nod, grinning. I wonder if maybe Jonah found in Brenda what I did; a woman with a whole lot of love to go around, who filled a hole that was left by the loss of his own mother.

"Well, I loved it so much that I asked her for the recipe, and she gave it to me."

I let out an impressed whistle. "She must like you. She'd rather cut off her own arm than give one of her recipes to someone she didn't think deserved it."

The music switches from upbeat Jazz to some slower piano tunes. I recognize a few of them from my Dad's old collections. We chit-chat our way through dinner, about Robbie and her books, Matt and their upcoming deals, Anna and Brenda, and how much we both adore them. Through some unspoken agreement, we both studiously avoid any of the heavier subjects that have come up between us over the past week.

"There's not much for dessert," he says as we bring our empty plates back into the kitchen. "Some ice cream, I think."

"I'll leave it," I say. "Thanks. I'm stuffed. I'll make some coffee, though. You have to be up super late, right?"

"Sure," he says. "That'd be great."

I turn around and open the cupboard, but all the cups that were in there yesterday are gone, apart from one set on the very top shelf that has been turned upside-down for storage.

I reach up, but even in my heels, I can only get the last knuckle of my middle finger over the edge of the shelf.

"I got it," says Jonah, suddenly behind me.

He reaches up, loops his forefinger through the handles of two mugs, and pulls them down.

"Thanks," I say, turning around.

I look up and smile at him, only to be struck dumb by the expression on his face. There have been fleeting moments this week where I thought he might want to kiss me, but nothing like this. There's no mistaking the look on his face at this moment; pure, undisguised desire.

I'm instantly ablaze, from the top of my head to the tips of my toes, and my heart flips when I hear the cups he was holding clatter onto the countertop.

"Franchesca, I—" he starts, and I sense that he's about to waver, to douse the sparks between us as he has so many times before, and leave me smoldering.

"I want to," I say quickly, before I can even stop myself.

Jonah lets slip a low groan—more of a conflicted, pained cry than a lustful moan. But his fingers slide along the side of my neck and he dips down, running the side of his nose slowly along the side of mine.

I tip my head and Jonah brushes his lips across mine. I can barely feel it, the touch is so soft and brief, but my body reacts as though I've been struck by lightning. I feel a tingling roll of arousal slip down my spine and a throb between my legs that makes me clench.

Jonah pulls back and looks at me, his nose barely a few inches from mine. His other hand comes to the other side of my neck, his fingers cool against my skin, his touch gentle as he cups my face and examines me like I'm a rare specimen.

"Franchesca," he whispers, and my eyelids droop with pleasure at the sound of my name.

He presses a kiss to the leftmost corner of my mouth, then the right. He pulls back again and runs his thumb over the soft pillow of my bottom lip, just like he did after he fed me whiskey the other night, and a little moan emanates from my throat.

I feel my nipples harden under my dress. My chest is buzzing with desire. I reach for him, my fingers curling a fist around the buttons of his shirt and pulling him toward me.

Jonah drops both his hands in unison and slides them around to the back of my thighs. He pulls me upward and uses his body to crowd me back onto the counter. I split my thighs and he surges in between them, his fingers back on my neck, cupping my face.

He moves slowly, trailing his lips over mine as his breaths comes fast and heavy. He looks like a starved man staring down a banquet, and yet he still won't give in to himself. Every time I try to pull him closer so he'll kiss me properly, he resists.

I slide my hips to the edge of the counter and groan when I feel the bulge in his pants pressing against me.

His tongue swipes over my lips, slowly and with intent, and then he finally presses his mouth to mine and urges my lips open with his own.

I bring my hand up over his chest, letting it glide across the cool linen and around his neck, lacing my fingers into the hair at his nape. His tongue probes my mouth and he teases me, pulling back and watching my face until I open my eyes in frustration, at which point he leans in and kisses me again.

"Jonah," I moan softly, pulling him closer.

He moves one arm to cup the back of my head, the other down to my hip and around to my ass, which he yanks forward, pulling me tighter against his hardness. I'm drowning in the pleasure of it, letting myself float in the intimacy of how slowly and how deliberately he explores the kiss. His hands move gently back over my body, towards my shoulders and the straps of the sundress. He loops one finger in each and begins drawing them slowly, slowly outwards towards the edge of my shoulders, the point where there'll be no turning back…

When suddenly, out of nowhere, a tinny version of the overture from *The Marriage of Figaro* starts blaring across the kitchen, and Jonah leaps away from me as though his mother just walked in on him with his prom date. I'm left sitting on the counter, the heat between my thighs cooling in the evening air where Jonah's body used to be.

It's such a bizarre intrusion that it takes me a moment to realize that the noise is Jonah's phone ringing. He shoots me an apologetic look that's mixed with something like shock, a hint of irritation, and maybe some regret, as he grabs the phone from the counter and puts it to his ear.

"Matt," he says, slightly out of breath.

I can't make out what Matt's saying on the other end of the phone but I can hear the muffled crackle of his voice against Jonah's ear.

"Yeah," says Jonah. "I was just working out."

Liar.

Realizing that Jonah is avoiding my eye, and assuming he's going to do one of his signature mood flips when he gets off the phone, I decide not to hang around. I do have *some* self-respect. I hop down from the counter and brush the front of my dress down into place.

"Yeah, I've been through the package today," Jonah is saying. Something about the Hong Kong call later, I guess. "I think I can bring them down ten percent. I can try for fifteen if you want."

He paces around to the other side of the kitchen island, presumably to get his now-awkward boner out of sight, and leans against it. He runs his hand through his hair in a gesture that looks very much like frustration.

I know how he feels. My lips are still tingling and my hair is a mess. I square my shoulders regardless and walk out of the kitchen into the hall that leads to my room. Jonah doesn't look at me. We both know the drill at this point. I'll be back at work next week anyway, and he'll be back with his lineup of supermodels. Best to just let it rest.

I pause for a moment to gather myself. My hands are shaking. I take three deep breaths, and let them out slowly between pursed lips.

"Haven't seen her all day," I hear Jonah saying, distantly.

He has to be talking about me. Who else would he be talking about on an island with a population of two? I roll

112

my eyes and start down the hall, resolving to leave Jonah to whatever game he's playing. But then he speaks again.

"I'm not going to do that, Matt."

Well, that has me curious enough to stay exactly where I am.

"Did you call me to talk about work, or to try and convince me to date your wife's friend again?" he asks, and his voice is suddenly cold and hard.

I feel a white-hot tide of embarrassment rise up in my chest. Is that what's been going on? Matt's been trying to get Jonah to date me, so he's been trying to play the part? And then every time he gets close to me, he realizes I'm not a supermodel playgirl and gets cold feet? It all makes sense now, and I feel so unbelievably stupid I can hardly stand it.

I take off down the hall at a run, forgetting that I have heels on. The noise of them click-clacking on the floor echoes around the house. Jonah must be able to hear it, but I don't care.

I explode into my room and slam the door behind me, leaning back against it, breathless. The flood of adrenaline —first from Jonah kissing me, then from the revelation that Matt's been trying to persuade him to get with me the whole time—is making me nauseous. Thank God I didn't manage to convince myself that Jonah had the potential to be anything more than a vacation fling. But the situation is still humiliating beyond words.

I do wonder briefly if Robbie had any idea that Matt was trying to cajole his business partner into pity-dating me, but I dismiss the thought immediately. There's no way. No way. And if she knew, she'd kill him.

I'm so annoyed, that I half-consider calling her to let her know what her husband has been up to. That would teach him not to meddle with other people. But considering that no harm has really been done, I calm down and manage to convince myself that it's not worth causing marital discord for my best friend. I'll wait until the next time I visit Meadow Hill and get him on his own to really bust his balls.

I take a shower to cool off, and it helps. Thirty minutes later, just as the sun is setting outside and I'm cracking open the book I swiped from the reading room, I hear a knock on the door. My heart leaps into my throat. I know Jonah's been flirting with me because Matt's been asking him to. Assuming he's not stupid, he knows I know, because he heard me running away from the kitchen. All of the blowing hot and cold stuff makes sense in hindsight. And I do not have a single shred of desire to talk about it right now.

"Franchesca?"

"I'm getting an early night," I call. And to forestall any reply he might have, and any attempt he might make to talk to me about it before we leave, I add "I'll be ready by five tomorrow."

I can't avoid him forever, but the likelihood is that I won't see him for the next several months, and by that time I'll have had a chance to give Matt a piece of my mind. That ought to put this whole awkward situation behind us.

"Right," Jonah says. There's a pause, then he repeats "Right," a little quieter this time, and I listen to his footsteps gradually disappear as he walks away down the hall.

Chapter 9

I get up early the next morning. Not because I'm especially well-rested, but because I kept waking up through the night with visions of Jonah and Matt laughing at me in my head, and eventually I decide that it's not worth trying to get back to sleep again.

I haven't been up for long before I notice that the air has lost its balmy feeling, and it's now thick with humidity. Every time I move, I start sweating, so I resolve to stop moving and instead spend the day out on the deck, soaking in the island before I have to leave it. I assume Jonah won't be up for ages anyway, since his meeting was at such an unreasonable hour, and I already have everything packed and ready to go.

I was planning on going for a swim in the sea, but the ocean looks a little rougher than usual. Jonah's seaplane is bobbing about beside the pier, higher than I've noticed it before.

A little before midday, just as I'm finishing the delicious fruit bowl I made myself for breakfast and have been picking at all morning, something happens that hasn't happened during the whole time I've been here: the sun is blotted out by a cloud.

The tropical breeze starts to rise gradually until it's an actual wind, lifting the pages of my book every now and then and making it difficult for me to read. And when a big, fat raindrop has the audacity to land in the very center of the page I'm reading, I decide to give up and finish my book inside, closing the door to the deck behind me.

My book of choice is *Pride and Prejudice*, which I've read a hundred times before, but the selection in the reading room is limited mostly to classics and a few paperbacks that people have left behind after vacations, and I've already been through all the more modern romance books that Robbie added to the collection.

Just as Elizabeth arrives at Rosings Park, I happen to glance up and notice that the weather outside has deteriorated even more. The wind is so strong that the palm trees are leaning over at an angle, their branches all fluttering in the same direction, and the rain is coming down in sheets. Jonah's plane is being jostled by the ocean so much that the wings occasionally dip into the waves, and the tide has risen to the point where I can no longer see the pier it's moored to.

I'm no expert, but it seems very much like weather we should not be attempting to fly in. Immediately, I feel a knot of tension in my gut. What if I can't get back to New York in time? Jessica isn't exactly the sort of boss who'd understand me being delayed by the weather.

It's almost 2pm according to my phone. Jonah's meeting didn't start until 3am, and I have no clue how long it went on. He seemed to have lots of prep material with him yesterday, so it could have been hours. I have no idea how long he'll be asleep.

Just as I manage to convince myself that it's better to let him sleep and speak to him when he wakes up, the lounger I was sitting on outside is lifted by the wind and rattles its way across the deck, slamming into the wall at the far end.

"Screw it," I say out loud, my heart beating a little faster. I set my book down and head through the house to the hall where the master bedrooms are. All the doors are open, the beds inside stripped back to mattresses by the staff, except for mine and one other.

"Jonah?" I call, rapping on the door with my knuckles.

No answer.

I knock again and hold my ear to the door. I think I can hear stirring inside, so I open the door a crack.

"Jonah?"

"Mmm?" he says, his voice cracking with sleep.

"Hey, sorry to bother you," I say. "I think there's a storm."

"S'just a little one," he says, sleepily. "It'll be gone by midday."

"Well, it's 2 pm and it looks like a big one," I tell him. "It's blowing sun loungers around outside."

There's a moment of silence, then I hear him shuffling on the sheets. A few seconds later the door is yanked from my hand, and Jonah stands there looking very sleepy and very hot in just his boxers.

"Hey," I say, taking a step back. He looks down at me, his eyes half-closed and his hair a scruffy mop on top of his head. I haven't seen him since the kitchen last night, and I had somehow managed, in my irritated state, to convince myself that he wasn't really that good-looking anyway.

That was a lie. Just an absolutely bald-faced lie.

"Hey," he says, scratching the back of his head. He brings his other arm up and stretches, and I have to look away.

"There was a storm forecast," he says. "I checked the weather last night. But it was supposed to be gone before lunchtime."

"Well, it's definitely not gone," I reply.

I feel like mentioning that he should have told me there was a storm due. It has ramifications for what clothes I would've chosen to wear today if nothing else. But I have bigger things to worry about. Like whether this is going to delay our flight home, and exactly how much of an earful I'm going to get from Jessica.

"Okay," says Jonah, stepping out into the hall. He moves ahead of me toward the kitchen, and I trail behind him, my head slightly tilted as I watch his butt cheeks rise and fall with every step.

Don't judge me, I can look. A hot guy with deep issues who's been blowing hot and cold in an effort to satisfy his friend's weird desire to set me up is still a hot guy.

"Woah," he says, stopping in his tracks as soon as he enters the kitchen and looks out the window. I almost walk right into his back. "Yeah, this wasn't supposed to happen."

"Will it delay us from getting home?" I ask.

He looks down at me like I'm crazy.

"Uh… yes. Yes, it will."

"God. Jessica's going to kill me," I say.

Jonah goes back to his room and reappears wearing some loose joggers and a tight blue t-shirt, with sneakers.

"What are you doing?" I ask.

"I have to tie a few things down," he says. "Get the loungers into storage so they don't smash the windows, and get the shutters closed."

"Well, what can I do?" I ask.

The displaced lounger outside drifts away from the wall and rattles against the metal pillar just beside the glass door.

"See what food you can find in the pantry that's ready to eat," he says, shaking out a thin waterproof jacket and pulling it over his head. "Bag it up. And there should be some flashlights in the cupboard right at the end."

His tone is completely even, but he sounds much more alert than just a moment ago, and what he's saying makes me think I might be in more trouble here than I realize. Just a few hours ago I was debating a swim in the sea.

"Okay," I say.

Jonah pulls the hood of his jacket up and tightens the drawstring, heading for the door.

"Hey, Jonah?" I call after him.

He turns to look at me.

"Please be careful."

He gives me a small smile and a nod, and then he's gone.

I rush into the pantry and find a bag, which I manage to fill with a selection of chips, crackers, and nut butters. I grab some cheese from the fridge and shove a few bottles of water into the bag for good measure. I don't really know what all this is for, but it's what Jonah asked for.

The flashlights aren't that hard to find. There are eight in total, but I only put two in the bag after I've checked that they work because I'm running out of space.

Once I've collected what Jonah asked me to, I return to the kitchen and go over to the window to see if I can spot him outside. There's a lot of banging, and the wind has started to howl eerily. The trees are leaning even farther than before, and the sea, which has been crystal blue for the whole week, now looks like dark gray soup.

I nearly jump right out of my skin when there's a loud banging on the window to my left. I look over with my hand on my chest, to see Jonah's face sporting an angry frown.

"*Get back!*" he shouts. I can barely hear his voice through the glass, especially with the noise of the wind, but I can't mistake his meaning when he gestures forcefully, pointing towards the room behind me.

"*Get away from the glass!*"

Ordinarily, I'd bristle at being told what to do, but he's so emphatic I find myself taking a couple of large steps backward before I even think about it.

Jonah lifts a metal flap on the wall beside him and hits a button, and metal shutters roll down over the windows all along both sides of the room, covering the glass and leaving me with only the dim artificial light inside.

It feels like I'm waiting an eternity for Jonah to return. I can still hear the howling wind and occasional banging and scraping outside, but I can't see anything now. If anything, it's even more anxiety-inducing.

I keep imagining what could have happened to him. Maybe he's been swept out to sea. Or chopped in half by a sun lounger, like something out of the *Final Destination* movies that Robbie, Anna, and I used to watch when Brenda was out. Maybe I'll be stranded here for months, surviving on peanut butter and posh wine until the yacht returns.

Suddenly, I'm startled by a loud bang at the side of the room. I spin around to see Jonah standing there, having finally returned through a side door to the kitchen that I hadn't even noticed before. He's breathless and dripping from head to toe, soaked through despite his jacket.

"Did you get everything done?" I ask.

"Pretty much," he says, stripping to his boxers again. He picks up the sodden pile of clothes and disappears down the hall.

While I'm waiting for him to change, I take a seat at the breakfast bar, pull out my phone, and try to send Sarah an email to let her know I might not be back in time. My phone blinks open a blank screen and tells me I have no internet connection.

"The internet's out," I tell Jonah when he returns in jeans and a thin sweater.

"It's satellite," he says. "And there are huge storm clouds over us."

"Ah," I say, slipping my phone back into my pocket. I nod toward the bag on the counter just beside me. "I got the stuff you asked for."

"Great," he says. He comes over to sit beside me and riffle through the bag, then gives a satisfied grunt.

Much to my surprise, he turns his chair around to face me. I glance up, notice he's watching me, and busy myself with trying to look like I'm reading something on my not-connected-to-anything phone.

"So, we definitely won't be flying back tonight?" I ask, without looking up, when the silence becomes too much to bear. Part of me just won't let it sink in that there's a chance I'll miss work on Monday.

Jonah is sitting in the chair beside mine, his hands in the pockets of his sweater and his feet on the rest bar that runs around the bottom of the breakfast bar. His thighs are wide apart, and he looks pretty relaxed, all things considered.

"Nope," he shakes his head.

I push up from the seat and curse under my breath. "Shit," I hiss, running my hand through my hair. I turn to glare at him. "How did you not know there was going to be a storm?"

Jonah lifts a brow slowly but answers me in a very level voice.

"I did know. It was forecast as a small storm, clearing by midday."

"Well, it didn't!" I say. My tone is accusatory, but all I can think of is that Jessica will jump all over this chance to make an example of me. I can already imagine Sarah explaining my downfall to the next poor soul who starts on hell year.

"It didn't," says Jonah, carefully, eyeing me quietly.

"Why didn't you just take me home yesterday?" I demand. "You would have been home in time for your meeting."

"Because I needed time to prepare, and…" he trails off.

"And *what?*" I demand.

"Nothing," he says.

"Well, thanks for *nothing*," I say. "*Nothing* is going to get me fired."

Somewhere deep down, I am aware that I'm being unreasonable. But my head is suddenly throbbing with stress as the reality of the situation starts to hit me. I'm not going to be back in time, Jessica may fire me, I'm on an island during a big tropical storm, and I'm alone with a man who's been reluctantly trying to fulfill his best friend's request to get it on with me. Good. God.

"Franchesca," says Jonah, suddenly beside me. His voice is quiet. Soothing, even. He reaches for my hand, and I yank it away from him and stare up at him, furious.

"Don't *Franchesca* me," I say. "You don't need to pretend to be into me anymore, okay? Frankly, I'm so stressed out that I can do without it."

So much for riding this out until I can tell Matt to back off.

Jonah's brow draws down. He looks genuinely confused, which is even more annoying than if he just acknowledged it.

"Franchesca," he says again, a little more firmly.

Well, screw him. I'm not playing his dumb games anymore.

He reaches for me again, and I dodge away from him before shoving my hand into the middle of his chest. It has the net effect of forcing *me* to take a step back because he's as solid as a wall.

"Stop!" I say, turning away.

I need to get away from him. From everything. I need space. And air. Without even thinking, I march the couple of steps between me and the side door, and turn the handle.

"*Francesca!*" His voice is different this time. Wilder. Frantic.

The last half of my name is drowned out by the wind, and my arm is nearly yanked out of its socket as the howling gale catches the door and yanks it open. I'm pulled just outside the room, and it's like stepping onto an alien planet. The wind is so strong I can't catch a breath. So strong I can *see* it blowing through the trees. Rain lashes at my face, and something big—I can't tell if it's a branch or something else—flies past me, about two inches in front of my face.

I feel a huge arm wrap around my middle and yank me backward, and I'm suddenly back inside, the door slamming behind me.

"You *idiot!*" Jonah shouts, setting me on my feet.

"I..." I say. He's not wrong. In my defense, it didn't seem like it would be *that* bad out there. The shutters are drowning out way more noise and calamity than I thought.

"You could have been *killed*," Jonah says, glaring down at me.

I suddenly feel very small and very stupid, and I don't like it one bit. So I square my shoulders and fold my arms.

"Well, at least then you wouldn't have to keep pretending to like me for the sake of Matt's stupid matchmaker attempts."

I storm forward a few steps, intent on going to my room to seethe until the storm passes, but just as I'm about to go past him, he reaches out and grabs me around the waist again, lifts me off my feet, and places me back where I was.

He folds his arms and stares down at me, placidly, and I glare back up at him, absolutely raging from my nose to my toes.

"You're obviously going through something," he says, calmly.

"Oh, come *on*," I snort. "I heard you on the phone! *Did you call me to talk about work, or to try and convince me to date your wife's friend again?*" I say, repeating Jonah's own words back to him while I wobble my head back and forth and do my best attempt at his deep voice.

Jonah looks like he's struggling to keep a straight face.

I storm past him again, and again he scoops me up and puts me back where I was.

"Stop it!" I say.

That's when the electricity goes out. We're plunged into pitch darkness, and in the absence of the quiet hum of idle appliances, the storm outside seems all the louder.

"It's getting worse," says Jonah. "Come on."

He reaches for me in the dark, somehow managing to grab my hand. I pull it away from him.

"We have to get to the shelter," he says. His voice is firm, and his tone is uncompromising. "I know you're pissed at me because you think you've got me all figured out, but if this storm picks up much more the shutters could give and the whole house after them. So, you are coming to the shelter with me. I can either lead you there by your hand, or I can throw you over my shoulder and carry you there. Up to you."

I'm quiet for a second, and then there's a loud crash from outside and my mind is made up. I reach out in front of me in the dark and find his arm still waiting there. He grabs me by the hand and pulls me along behind him. I'm reminded of the scavenger hunt, but he's blind here, too, and the stakes are much higher.

He knows his way around the place so well that we cross to the breakfast bar in a matter of seconds. There's a quiet rustle and a click, and Jonah's face lights up suddenly with the light from one of the flashlights.

"This way," he says, and leads me through to the pantry. Once we're inside, he drops my hand and bends down. There's a small catch on the floor that I hadn't even noticed before. He releases the catch, which causes a square portion of the floor to lower an inch with a hydraulic hiss, and then he's able to slide it across to reveal a hole in the floor. When he shines his flashlight down into it, I can see steps leading downward.

"Here," he says, handing me the flashlight. "You go first."

"What's down there?" I ask, taking the flashlight from him and moving closer to the hole.

"A wine cellar and a storm bunker," he says. "Just go straight down, through the cellar, and you'll see the bunker door at the far end."

"What about you?" I ask. I'm still mad at him, but I don't want to be alone.

"I'm just going to close the hatch back over and then I'll be along behind you. You can wait for me if you don't want to go alone."

I step around Jonah and lower myself tentatively onto the wooden steps. It's solid, with no give under my foot at all. When I reach the bottom there's a short hall that opens into a big wine cellar full of bottles. Sure enough, when I shine the light in front of me there's a door about ten feet away.

I turn around and see Jonah at the top of the stairs, twisted around with his sweater slightly ridden up to reveal a sliver of his stomach. He pulls the trapdoor across, and a moment later I see the light from the other flashlight when he switches it on.

We head for the door at the end of the wine cellar, and Jonah pushes it open.

"Oh," I say, stepping inside.

The storm shelter is, of course, way more comfortable than I imagined. I don't know why I'm surprised that billionaires ride out storms in double-wide, bouncy armchairs, but I am.

Each chair is a different shade of gray or blue, or gray-blue, and has a slightly different design. There are eight in total, and a couple of them are folded out into beds. There's a small kitchen in the corner, and a shelving unit with a handful of books and some board games on it.

"Are you claustrophobic?" asks Jonah, right beside my ear.

"No," I say, and move into the room, dropping into one of the big chairs and kicking off my sliders.

"Just as well," he says.

He moves over to the kitchen and unloads the bag in his hand, but I can see that my supplies are unnecessary. There's already plenty of food in the pantry cupboard, and five full stacks of bottled water.

He reaches into a different cupboard and pulls out a large box with a handle on top, and when he sets it down, I can see that it's a large power bank, like the type people take camping when they're going to be off-grid for a few days. He sets it on the table, pulls a charging cable out of the same cupboard, and connects up a lantern light, making our flashlights obsolete. I click mine off and put it on the small table beside my chair.

"How long will that thing last for?" I ask, nodding toward the power bank.

"If we only use the light?" he says. "About three days. But the storm won't last that long. You can use the kettle and the stove if you want to."

Jonah switches off his own flashlight and sits down in the chair directly opposite me.

I remain stubbornly silent, still feeling a little stupid for walking outside earlier, and feeling irritated about feeling stupid. And worried about what will happen when I get home. And annoyed that Jonah didn't even try to apologize for his and Matt's behavior before the lights went out. All in all, I could be having a much better day.

Jonah doesn't say anything either. He sits in his chair, feet flat on the floor, his arms resting idly at his sides, staring at me intently. After what seems like an eternity, he takes a breath.

"So…"

Chapter 10

I glare at Jonah. "So what?" I snap.

"So, do you want to talk about what you think you know?"

"I don't *think* I know anything," I say. "I know what I heard."

Jonah considers me in silence.

"It's fine anyway. It's not like I was under any illusions that…" I trail off. "I was only thinking it might be a fun vacation fling, Jonah," I say, opting for honesty. "It's *you* that kept blowing hot and cold. Even back at the wedding. And I don't need Matt's pity setups. And I don't like being made to feel like some pitiful desperado chasing you down when *you're* the one who's instigated every time we… And if I'd known that was why you were doing it…"

I stop and take a deep breath, and sigh it out. That was quite a cathartic rant. I'm actually feeling a bit better now.

"Well, anyway," I say. "I'm sorry I acted like that upstairs. I'm a bit stressed."

I look across at Jonah. He's looking back at me in silence like he's taking in everything I just said.

"To be clear," he says after a while. "You think I kissed you yesterday because Matt's been pestering me to date you?"

"Mmm," I confirm with a nod of my head.

"And why do you think he'd do a thing like that?"

I shrug. "Maybe because he's Robbie's husband, and she's probably told him that I've dated a lot but never met anyone I really liked, and he thinks he's doing a nice thing for his wife and her friend," I reply. "That's the most charitable explanation I can come up with."

"I see," says Jonah.

He falls quiet again, and after a moment I lean my head back against the chair and close my eyes. I can feel the beginnings of a tension headache coming on, and I don't want it to get any worse.

"What if he was *telling* me to make a move because he knew I wanted to?" Jonah asks suddenly. He almost blurts it, which is the first time I've heard him blurt anything.

I snort. "Come on, Jonah. I don't believe for a second you need any convincing to make a move."

"I don't make moves," he says. "As a rule."

"Then how come you date so much?"

"I don't date," he says, resolutely.

I can so scarcely believe my ears that I actually let out a little laugh. "What the hell are you talking about? I've seen pictures of you with enough models to run your own London Fashion Week."

130

"They're friends," he says. "And they keep me off those dumb eligible bachelor lists that Matt was always on before he met Robbie."

"But… why?" I ask.

"Why don't I want to be on dumb eligible bachelor lists?"

"No. Why don't you date?"

"I'm busy," he says.

"Bullshit," I say, shaking my head. I lean forward, suddenly intrigued. He's become a puzzle. "That's not it. Matt's busy, too, but he managed to get with Robbie. And you're not afraid to flirt. You flirted with me the first time I ever met you. You're pretty forward, actually."

He lifts his brows but doesn't say anything.

"I mean, I get why *I* don't date. Dating apps are a dumpster fire. But you're a super-hot billionaire," I say. "You're successful, handsome… I mean, obviously, you know all this because you know you'd be on the eligible bachelor lists if people thought you weren't dating."

"I honestly can't tell if I'm being complimented or insulted," he says. "Are you going to spend the whole night trying to analyze me?"

"Maybe," I say. "It's not every day you get stranded on a tropical island with a celibate billionaire."

"I didn't say that," he says.

"What?"

"I didn't say I was celibate. I said I don't date."

"Riiiight," I say slowly, as the plot thickens. "So… you don't date."

Jonah nods.

"But you do have one-night stands?"

He nods again. "Occasionally."

"But Matt was trying to convince you to make a move on me because you told him you wanted to?"

He closes his eyes and sighs.

"Look. For reasons I won't go into, I don't date. And I haven't for years. I happened to mention to Matt that *if* I was going to date someone, I'd date you. And he hasn't shut up about it since."

"Oh," I say again. I'm not quite sure how I feel about this. It's like hearing the best compliment I've ever been paid, followed immediately by a "*but…*"

"Well, what about me?" I say.

Jonah looks over at me and raises a brow.

"Don't I get a say?" I ask. "It seems pretty unfair that you and Matt are deciding all this without any input from me."

"It's not like that," he says.

"What if I don't date either?" I ask. "I'm pretty busy, too, you know?"

"Stop it," says Jonah, without a hint of humor on his face.

"What?" I ask, wearing my most innocent expression.

"You're about to tell me that you wouldn't mind if I just fucked you," he says. Which is exactly what I was about to say, but hearing him say it instead makes my heart skip a beat.

"So what if I am?" I ask. Call me cruel, but the fact that he has literally nowhere to run this time, after the number of times he's cut out on me before, gives me a little thrill.

"I don't want to just fuck you," he practically snarls. "You're stepping on dangerous territory here, Franchesca."

"You don't want to?" I ask, tilting my head quizzically.

He stares at me through the dim light from the lantern. His expression is the same as it was in the kitchen the night before, but somehow even more intense. I can almost feel the heat emanating from him, and I'm reveling in the effect I can have on him in here, stuck in this bunker with me. He's like a caged animal, and I'm a stick to prod him with.

"I want to," I say.

He takes a deep, long breath and rolls his eyes up to the heavens. His breathing is slightly labored.

"I don't have any protection in here," he says, through gritted teeth.

"I'm on birth control," I reply.

"I don't date," he says.

"Me neither," I lie.

"If you ask again, I'm going to lose my self-control," he tells me plainly.

A silence falls between us. It's so quiet down here, you'd never guess there was a huge storm raging overhead. Jonah stares at me and I stare at him, letting the silence linger. I already know exactly how to push him over the edge, to make him lose that last little bit of self-control, and I debate with myself whether or not I should pull the trigger.

133

"Please?" I whisper.

He surges from his chair as quick as a panther, closing the gap between us in less than a second. Before I have time to think, his lips are on mine, his hand is on the back of my head, and he has my hand in his, pulling me to my feet.

I kiss him back, suddenly, undeniably full of lust. I push up onto the tips of my toes and sling my arms around his neck.

"You're sure?" he asks, pulling out of the kiss for a moment and searching my face. "Last chance."

"Yes," say. "I'm sure."

He dips down and picks me up, one arm behind my legs and the other behind my back, and kisses me as we make our way over to one of the beds. I expect him to lay me down, but instead, he places my feet on the mattress so I can stand on it. In this position, I'm almost exactly at eye-level with him, maybe slightly higher.

I lean down to kiss him. We both know there's no backing out or running away anymore, and that reality seems to have liberated Jonah. He keeps his hands on my hips to steady me on the mattress and runs his gaze up and down my body, making no effort anymore to hide his desire. I'm wearing a tank top and a pair of shorts—hardly the most seductive outfit—but he doesn't seem to care in the least.

"Are your nipples sensitive?" he asks.

I flush immediately and bite my bottom lip. I'm not sure I've ever been asked so directly before.

"Yes," I whisper, my throat tight. I can feel my nipples hardening under my tank and bra, and when I look down at Jonah there's a slight smile tugging at one corner of his mouth as he looks directly at my breasts.

He slides his hand up my side and extends his thumb to sweep across the small bump of my nipple.

"Even through your clothes?" he asks.

I feel like my knees are going to buckle.

"Yes," I say.

He rubs his thumb in small circles around my nipple and lifts his head to look up at my face.

"You like that, Franchesca?" he asks.

"Mmm," I moan.

He moves his hand across my chest and rolls his thumb around my other nipple. Waves of wanting undulate through my belly and coalesce between my thighs.

"And this?"

"Yes," I whisper quickly.

Jonah slides his hands down my arms and brings my hands up to his shoulders, where I place them to steady myself now that he's let go of my hips.

He puts the tips of his fingers under the bottom of my tank and trails his warm skin along mine as he pushes the top up, over my breasts, until it sits gathered above my bra.

My heart is beating so hard in my chest that I can hear it thrum loudly in my ears.

Jonah runs his touch over my nipples again, this time with one less layer of cloth under his fingers. He takes them both between his thumbs and forefingers, gently squeezing.

I moan, my knees buckling slightly. I hadn't expected him to take his time with me like this, and it's such perfect torture that I'm not sure how much I can stand.

"You like this?" he asks.

"Yes," I say, urgently.

"Harder?" he asks. His voice is a little deeper than before.

"Yes," I say, arching my back slightly.

He adds a little pressure, and I feel my nipples harden even more.

"Harder?" he asks.

"Yes," I say.

"Then ask," he tells me, holding the pressure exactly as it is.

"Harder," I breathe.

The squeezing becomes a pinch, and I gasp. Jonah eases off a little, gives me time to recover, then pinches again until I moan.

"More," I say. There's an urgency in my voice I've never heard before, and he hasn't even taken off my bra yet. I'm starting to understand why he gave me so many opportunities to back out, even if I'd rather die than stop now.

He hooks his thumbs under the bottom of my bra and pulls it upward, freeing my breasts, and letting the bra settle at the top of my chest with my tank.

"Beautiful," he breathes, pulling back a little to get a better look at me. I feel somehow more exposed with my bra pulled up than I would if he'd taken it off entirely.

He presses the flat of his tongue against my sensitive nipple, pulling a gasp from my mouth and causing me to curl my fingers into his shoulders. He rolls his tongue over the hard little bump, flicks it, and then he blows air softly onto my wet skin. Tendrils of pleasure snake all around me.

"Oh my God," I whisper.

He does the same on the other side, and then puckers his lips and sucks my nipple into his mouth, flicking his tongue against the tip.

I'm not expecting a touch on my belly, so when I feel his fingers there, I gasp and flinch, then laugh out the tension.

"Sorry," I say, softly.

There's a little *pop* as he pulls back, letting the suction break around my nipple, and looks up at me.

"I'm going to pull your shorts down," he says.

I swallow hard and nod.

"And I'm going to see how wet you are."

I can't speak. My entire body is tight and coiled and buzzing with need. I nod again.

Jonah uses both hands to peel my shorts down my legs. I move to step out of them, but he stops me.

"No," he says, placing a hand on the outside of my thigh. "Leave them there."

I obey, leaving my shorts around my ankles, and much like the bra that's still sitting at the top of my chest, it somehow makes me feel *more* naked.

"Do you feel aroused, Franchesca?" Jonah asks me.

"Yes," I say.

"Wet?" he asks.

I nod.

I feel his fingers slide against my mons and down along the gusset of my underwear. My hips tilt forward without any conscious intent from me.

"My God," he smiles wickedly. "You're like a furnace down here."

I feel myself clench with need, right against his hand, and he sucks a lustful hiss through his teeth. He presses his thumb against the purple cotton of my panties, running it back and forth along my lips gently.

"Do you have any idea how beautiful you look right now?" he asks.

I look down at him. I feel like my eyes are half glazed over. I can barely think, never mind answer him. The first thing that comes to mind is what tumbles out of my mouth.

"More," I say.

Jonah presses his thumb upward, pushing the material of my panties up through my lips and against my clitoris.

"More?" he asks as I flinch at his touch. It sends a shock of pleasure right through me, and I answer him with a lascivious groan.

"Yes," I breathe.

"Ahh, there it is," he croons. I don't even need to ask what he means. I can feel the wetness between my thighs. I already know it's seeped through my panties.

Jonah's fingers curl around the sides of my underwear and pull downwards, but he stops at my knees instead of pulling them all the way off.

"Look," he tells me.

I meet his gaze.

"Look at yourself. Look how wet your panties are."

I steady myself on his shoulders and look down.

I see my shorts around my ankles, my panties suspended across my knees, with a big, clear damp patch on them, and then my body fully exposed right up to where my bra and top sit at the top of my chest.

"Don't you look hot?" Jonah asks me, his fingers back between my legs. He dips his middle finger in between my lips and drags it forward until he finds my clitoris, and starts to move his finger around it in torturously slow circles.

"Yes," I admit, but it comes out half a strangled moan.

He toys with me slowly, watching every gasp and moan play out on my face as he circles, lightly coaxing me further and further down a path of madness, dizzying my mind with little flicks of his tongue against my nipples.

"Let me touch you," I whisper.

"Not yet, baby," he tells me. "I want to see you pop first."

He keeps stroking me, circling my ever-more sensitive bud with the same rhythm, over and over, and I find myself leaning onto him, my head resting on his shoulder as I moan and pant beside his ear.

"Good girl," he says, as my legs start to shake.

I grab tightly around his neck and cling to him, and my hips buck and roll as the pleasure starts to build deep in the pit of my stomach, tendrils traveling to wrap around every inch of my body.

"Oh, my God," I breathe. My voice is high-pitched and desperate. I barely recognize it.

Jonah laces his fingers into my hair and makes a fist, pulling my head from his shoulder and smothering my lips with his, probing my mouth with his tongue in a rhythm that matches the way his fingers perform on my sex.

My legs shudder underneath me. I feel the pressure reach an impossible pitch inside me, filling me with an almost-pleasure that is reaching and reaching but never quite satisfying, until I finally approach the precipice and tumble over, my hips bucking, my abdomen rolling through wave after wave of tensing, clenching pleasure. I moan loud into Jonah's mouth, grinding on his hand, and he pulls me closer, plunging his tongue between my lips as though seeking to find more of those sounds and pull them from me.

As my orgasm subsides, Jonah guides me down from the bed, still dazed. He pulls the tank and bra gently over my head and the panties the rest of the way down my legs, letting me step out of them.

"Lay down," he says quietly.

I still can't think straight or make head nor tail of the best orgasm I've ever had in my life, so I do as he asks.

I lay there with my head on the fluffy pillow, completely naked, and watch Jonah as he pulls his sweater over his head and unbuttons his jeans. When he turns to the side, I can see his erection straining against his boxers. He grabs a blanket from a pile on another chair, lays down behind me, and drapes the blanket over the two of us.

"Are you good?" he asks, slinging his arm around me.

"Mmm," I say, lazily. "But it's your turn now."

"Shh," he says. "Relax a while. We have all night."

I guess he's right. I lay my head back down and snuggle back against him, pulling his arm tighter around me and enjoying the warmth. God knows what's happening over our heads. We have no clue if the house is even still standing. But down here, everything is just perfect.

$\sim$

I stir awake from a sleep I hadn't meant to fall into and stretch, only remembering where I am and what just happened when Jonah pulls me closer to him.

"Hey, sleepyhead," he says.

"Oh, God," I say. "How long was I asleep?"

"Not long," he says. "Maybe an hour."

I breathe a sigh of relief. That's not as bad as falling asleep all night, at least.

"Sorry," I say.

"What for?" he asks, amusement in his voice.

"Well for coming and then falling asleep right after. At least now you know how women feel."

I look over my shoulder to see him grinning.

"I'm glad I wore you out so much," he says.

"You can wear me out any time you like, if it's gonna be like that," I tell him.

He reaches up and pushes some stray hairs out of my face.

"Don't tempt me," he says.

"I actually think things work out quite well when I tempt you," I say, wriggling backward to press my ass against him, very intentionally.

"Are you always this insatiable?" he asks.

I look over my shoulder and grin at him. "Only when I have a debt to pay."

Truth is, I'm really never this comfortable with a man. Something about Jonah has always lulled me into a sense of security, no matter how many times he's pulled away from me. Maybe now that he's explained the *why* a bit more—even if his explanation doesn't fully make sense to me—those days are finally gone.

"Oh, yeah," he says, pretending to have forgotten. "That's right."

He slides his hand down my belly and between my legs, cupping my sex. I feel him grow hard against my behind, springing to life almost instantly, and I reach back to stroke him.

"Oh, well that's no good!" I say.

"What?"

"You have clothes on."

A chuckle rumbles through his chest, and he rolls away from me slightly to remove his boxers. When he rolls back, I can feel his bare skin against mine. I reach back again and close my fist around his length, drawing a soft groan from him.

"You're so hard," I say, running my fist up and down the length of his cock.

He slides his hand down past my belly again and slips his finger between my folds. I flinch, still sensitive from earlier, and arch my back slightly.

"Is it okay?" he whispers.

"Yes," I tell him, already feeling my body heating up again, tingles reaching down each of my limbs.

"You still want me to fuck you?" he asks.

"Yes," I whisper, slightly breathless already.

I feel his length twitch in my hand, and he somehow gets even harder.

"Tell me," he says.

"I want you to fuck me, Jonah," I say, tightening my grip on his cock.

He removes his hand from between my legs and takes mine from his length, sliding it up and over my head as he pushes me onto my belly.

I lay on my front, stretched out underneath him, and he trails his fingers down my sides, making me giggle as he moves over my ribs and sends a tickle shooting through my body.

His knees are planted on either side of my thighs, and I can feel the measure of his arousal resting against me.

He slides a finger down from behind me, and straight into my slick entrance. I lift my backside up a little to ease his path and moan quietly at the feeling of him inside me.

"Tell me again," he says, his voice gravelly.

"I want you to fuck me," I say. I'm surrounded by the heady scent of my own sex mingled with the masculine cologne he wears, and all my troubles, from the raging storm outside to Jessica's inevitable wrath, might as well be worlds away for all I care about them right now.

Jonah extracts his finger from within me, and then I feel him push into me again, this time with two fingers. He hooks them inside me slightly, pressing down against my front wall, asserting a pressure that makes me instantly breathless as he circles that very spot in a steady rhythm.

"Again," he coaxes, his other hand on my back, rubbing a soothing path up and down my spine.

"I want you to fuck me," I repeat, this time much more insistently. "I want to feel you inside me, Jonah."

This seems to be all the persuasion he needs. He withdraws his fingers again and shifts his weight upward, lining up his tip with my entrance.

"I'll go slow," he tells me. "Tell me when you're ready for more, okay?"

I nod, though right now I can barely stand the anticipation.

He presses forward, and a shudder runs right through me as he enters. I feel myself stretching, opening up for him. There's a little pain— it's been a long time for me—but it's overwhelmed by an intense pleasure and relief, as anticipation gives way to reality. He stops when he's about an inch inside me; I take a few deep breaths and wiggle my hips up and down, adjusting myself to him.

"More," I say, and he pushes in another inch. I can hear his breathing getting heavier as he goes deeper, and it seems more and more like he's struggling to maintain control of himself.

"More," I say, quickly. He slides in another inch, and shifts his weight again, placing a hand down on each side of my shoulders.

He's so close to me now, I can hear every little hitch of his breath when I move my hips, and the deep, guttural groans when I clench around him.

"You're killing me, Franchesca," he says beside my ear.

"I want all of it," I say.

With a deep groan of pleasure, he pushes forward the rest of the way until he's hilted inside me, and I can feel him stretching and filling every bit of room I have to give. He drops down to his elbows, laying on top of me without making me bear any of his weight, and breathes steadily.

"Tell me when you're good," he says.

"I'm good," I tell him.

He pulls out of me, almost all the way, and slides back into me slowly until he hilts again. He somehow manages to find the exact spot inside me that he was pressing with his fingers just a minute ago, and I feel myself almost melt into the bed.

"More," I breathe.

He pulls out of me and slides back in with a more fluid motion this time, and hisses a "*Fffuck*" beside my ear.

145

His hands find mine. He laces his fingers between my own and dips his head, panting and groaning quietly beside my ear as he picks up a slow and steady rhythm. I lay underneath him, gasping every time he slides back into me.

"I want you to come inside me," I pant, and the strangled groan of lust he lets out almost makes me come again.

He moves his hips faster, picking up the pace until the room is filled with the sound of skin slapping skin, and with my moans, and with his grunts and pants, and the carnal scent of sex.

I can feel the pleasure building again, different this time. It starts in the pit of my stomach but somehow creeps all the way up my spine and into my head, growing in intensity as Jonah ruts himself into me.

When the peak comes, it feels different again. It explodes all of a sudden, shattering me into vibrating, incoherent shards. I scream as the pleasure crashes through me, wave after wave, each of them robbing me of whatever control I had before. I feel myself clench around Jonah's length, as deep as he can get and still pushing, as though he's trying to burrow into my very core. As I clench, again and again as the waves roll over me, he reaches his own climax and lets out something between a groan and a roar as he spills inside me, filling me.

He stills, breathing heavily beside my ear and slowly rolling his hips back and forth. We're both in the dreamy post-coitus time now, our bodies twitching and sensitive as they adjust back to normality. Every time I clench involuntarily around him, he groans softly and his hips buck reflexively. He still doesn't stop, though. He stays inside me as long as he can, until I feel him starting to soften, and he's forced to pull out.

I shuffle over and drape myself onto his torso with a satisfied sigh. He pulls me closer to him and plants a kiss on the top of my head.

We lay there in silence for a while, catching our breath while he strokes my hair and I trail little patterns over his chest with the tip of my finger.

"We should have done that last week," I say, quietly.

"Last year," says Jonah, and lets out a sigh.

We resolve to sleep in the bunker. We say it's because the storm is more likely to have passed by morning, but really I just don't think either of us wants to leave this moment until we have to. So we curl up together on the bed, our bodies entwined, and I fall into the most peaceful sleep I've had in a very, very long time.

Chapter 11

I have no idea what time it is when I wake up. The room is pitch black, and the only thing I can hear is the slow, steady rhythm of Jonah's breathing.

I stretch out my arm to see if I can reach the lantern on the table, and Jonah stirs behind me. His arm is already draped over me, but as he regains consciousness he sneaks it around my belly and pulls me close.

"Good morning, beautiful," he says.

"Hey," I say.

"What time is it?" he asks.

"I don't know. I was just trying to get the lantern so I can find my phone."

"Oh," he says, "it's over here. I took it to the bathroom while you were asleep."

He stretches away from me, and I moan a sad little noise at the sudden rush of cool air against my back.

"Alright, alright," he says, chuckling.

He hits the button on the lantern to turn it on, then rolls back toward me, wrapping me up in his arms once again.

"I had a cat like you when I was growing up," he says. "Always complaining when I tried to move."

I try to imagine Jonah as a cat person. For some reason, I hadn't imagined him as a pet person at all, but if I did, he would definitely have been a dog person.

"You didn't complain last night," I grin cheekily at him, "when you were making me purr."

Jonah kisses my shoulder. "I'll never get tired of that."

I try to ignore the way his response hints at the future. Incredible sex does not necessarily make great relationship material, and there's still a distinct possibility nagging at the back of my mind that once we're out of the confines of the bunker, he could go all cold shoulder again. Plus, I wasn't really lying when I said I was too busy to date. Especially someone who lives in an entirely different city.

Now that I can see, I lean forward and pick my phone up from the table.

"It's midday," I say. "But I still have no signal."

I reluctantly shift away from Jonah and turn over so I can see his face. He's frowning, his lips pursed in thought.

"What?" I ask.

"Well," he says, "that could just mean there's no signal in here. I've never had to come down here before, so I don't know."

"Or?" I ask.

"Or it could mean the storm is still raging," he says. "Which would be very unusual for this time of year. Or it could mean the storm has passed but it's done a lot of damage."

I groan. As amazing as last night was—and trust me when I say that it was better than I'd ever imagined it could be—I have to return to reality at some point. And the reality is, if I don't get back to work by Monday, Jessica is going to revel in making my life a misery—and that's the best-case scenario, assuming she doesn't just straight-up fire me.

"You worried about your awful boss?" he asks.

"What else?" I ask.

"She can't be that bad," he says, way too optimistically. He must be sex drunk.

"Seriously?" I say, "think of the most neurotic sorority girl you ever met at one of your elite colleges."

He looks upward, thinking. His eyebrows lift as though a particularly unpleasant memory has just come back to him, and he nods.

"OK," I say. "Now imagine her 15 years later, within reaching distance of her dream job. And then imagine that dream job is promptly given to a friend of the company owner's son."

"Rough," says Jonah. "And almost always terrible for the business."

"Right," I say. "Now give her interns to torture."

He exhales sharply. "Yikes."

"Yes," I nod, glad that we're finally on the same page. "She's really capable and works her ass off, she's just in no way a people person. But if I can get through this year, I'll be on the right track. And if I earn my accreditation at AJX, then I can work anywhere."

"Addison's like that," Jonah says. "Our head of business architecture. Amazingly talented, but absolutely no time for anyone who isn't on her level."

"Does she torture interns, too?" I ask.

"No," says Jonah, rolling away from me and getting to his feet. "But Matt and I wouldn't make a nepotistic hire and waste her talents. No wonder she's pissed all the time."

I roll over on the bed to watch him dress, mulling over what he said. I guess he has a point. I almost feel sympathetic for Jessica, until I remember that I am the tortured intern in this scenario.

"I'm going to check what's happening up top," he says.

"I'll come with you," I tell him, pushing myself up and stretching my arms into the air. The blanket falls down around my waist, and when I look back up, Jonah is staring at me hungrily.

"You're going to have to stop," he says. "Or we'll never leave this room, and all our family and friends will be traumatized for life when they get back here in a few weeks and find our skeletal remains fused at the pelvis."

I grin at him and make a face like I'm struggling to weigh up the options. He snorts a laugh and throws my tank top in my face.

The house is still standing, at least. Everything is eerily still as we emerge from the trap door. Jonah takes my hand and helps me up the last few steps, and we walk through the pantry into the kitchen. He goes straight for the console at the far end of the room, on the wall just next to the big panel windows, and flips a switch.

The shutters start to rise, slowly and very creakily, and natural light—bright, streaming sunlight, I quickly realize—bathes the room. Jonah comes over to stand beside me and survey the scene outside.

There is some damage that's pretty evident at a glance. A few trees have broken off halfway down their trunks and are lying at weird angles along the beach, and the canopy that was folded away on the deck, just above the windows, is only connected on one side, with the other end touching the floor.

"Doesn't look *too* bad," I say, glancing up at Jonah.

He's staring out of the window with a frown.

"Mmm," he says.

"What's wrong?" I ask.

He lifts his hand and points out toward the ocean.

"You see that white dot on the horizon?" he asks.

I squint, following the direction he's pointing in and scanning the horizon until I see it.

"Yeah," I say.

"I'm pretty sure that's my plane."

I gasp. I hadn't even realized that his plane wasn't on the pier anymore.

"Oh my God," I say, panic rising suddenly in my chest. "How are we going to get home?"

I lift up my phone and swipe at the screen. Still no service or internet connection.

This cannot be happening, I think to myself.

"This *cannot* be happening," I repeat aloud, striding across the room. I stop beside the lighting panel and hit every switch up and down. Nothing.

Jonah is still standing where he was, arms folded loosely in front of his chest, watching me.

"How can you be so calm?" I demand.

"What's the alternative?" he asks, calmly.

It's a fair point. My shoulders slump with a sigh and I huff back against the wall.

"Relax," he says. "Someone will come for us."

"That's it?" I say, staring at him with disbelief. "That's your plan? Just wait for someone to come and collect us?"

He purses his lips like he's trying to think of an alternative, then nods his head. "Pretty much, yup."

"What about your plane?"

"Well, I can't swim that far," he says, gesturing out to the distant little dot bobbing on the horizon. "So unless you're offering to go get it, I guess we'll see if we can salvage it after we're picked up."

"What about your deal in Manhattan?

"Pretty sure they'll understand that this situation was unavoidable," he says, tilting his head at me. He's starting to look amused, which is incredibly sexy and unbelievably infuriating. "I'll reschedule."

"So, what?" I ask, sarcasm thick in my voice. "You're going to LARP as Robinson Crusoe and make friends with a coconut and just hope someone will randomly stop by this extremely isolated private island in the middle of the ocean to rescue you?"

"No," he says, calmly. "When I don't arrive at the airport on time, my driver will know something's up. He'll check the flight logs and realize I never left the island. Then he'll probably give the company a heads-up, and when they can't get in touch with me, someone—probably Addison— will figure out that it's because of the *huge storm right over the island* that was ten times worse than forecast. And then someone—probably Matt's pilot, since he's not using his plane right now, or possibly the coast guard—will be sent out to check up on us."

"Oh," I say, deflating. That all sounds very reasonable.

"Yes, I'm irritatingly sensible," he says, definitely amused now. And then, after a beat, he adds "It was a volleyball, by the way."

I'm so perplexed by this that I suddenly forget I'm supposed to be angry and scared. "A what?"

"It was a volleyball that Tom Hanks made friends with in that movie. Not a coconut. You can get angry at me all you want, but I'll thank you to leave Wilson out of this."

He stands there with a grin plastered across his face. I stare at him for a few seconds, and then I can't help myself—I burst out laughing.

"I'm going to see if I can figure out what's up with the power and comms," he says, still grinning. "And then I'm going to see if I can fuck you in every room in this house before anyone gets here."

I swallow hard, my heart suddenly fluttering behind my sternum like a captive bird. I guess he hasn't gotten cold feet since leaving the bunker, after all. Quite the opposite, in fact.

"I mean," he continues nonchalantly, "if that's alright with you, and you don't have any other plans?"

"Su—" I cut off as my voice cracks, and stop to clear my throat. "Sure," I say, nodding. "Yeah. No plans here."

The left side of his mouth lifts into a smirk.

"I won't be long," he says, and heads out.

∾

I spend the rest of the afternoon trying to find something to do. I could read more of my book, but that would just make me feel lazy when Jonah is outside trying to fix everything.

I decide to take a shower—I could use it after last night's… *activities*—but the water won't turn hot even after five minutes of letting it run. The pool is full of floating debris from the storm, so I can't go in there.

I haunt the halls of the house for an hour or so, walking into every vacant bedroom and marveling at how the other half lives. It's been a vacation for me, but this isn't just somewhere that Jonah and Matt come for a week of relaxation once a year. They own it. They can come here whenever they want. And as Jonah proved the night before last, they can even work from here if they want to. I imagine Robbie, sitting in the library surrounded by books as she writes her own, and the thought of it makes me smile.

I'm still tempted to pick up a book as I pass through the reading room, but I resist. Jonah is still busy trying to get the power back on. He's stomped through the house a few times, each time with a different tool in hand, looking increasingly flustered and annoyed, so I've mostly tried to stay out of his way.

I head down to the bunker to fold up the blankets and strip the sheets from the bed we slept on last night. I put all our trash in a bag, gather the half-empty bottles of water, and grab the power bank to bring back upstairs—just in case.

"No faith in me, huh?" asks Jonah, who is topless in the kitchen, smeared in sweat and grease and wiping his hands in a clean towel. He nods at the power bank in my hands.

"Oh, this? I just brought it up so we can recharge it when you definitely succeed at fixing the power any minute now," I say.

Jonah chuckles, shaking his head. "Nice recovery," he says.

"So, still no luck?"

"No," he says. "I've tried everything I can think of. I'll leave it for today. The power bank should have enough juice left in it to get us through the night."

I sigh heavily. "I guess I should just accept that I'm not going to make it to work on Monday," I say. "And Jessica is going to make my life hell for the next eight months."

"Which company is it you're interning at again?" Jonah asks.

"AJX Marketing," I say.

"Oh," says Jonah, his brows raising. "I know Jimmy."

"Who?" I ask.

"Jimmy… James Hobson," he says.

"Oh!" I say. James Hobson is the CEO of AJX. "Of course you do."

Of course he does.

"Remember the other day when I told you a well-known marketing CEO nearly drowned during one of Matt's games and I had to rescue him?"

"Yeah."

"That was Jimmy."

"Really?" I ask with a laugh. "What the hell was he doing playing one of Matt's games?"

"No idea," says Jonah, shrugging. "He was here for a business thing and I guess he had one too many daiquiris. I can call him for you if you want. Tell him it's my fault you're held up."

I raise a brow at him. "Are you insane? Jessica's going to be pissed enough that I missed a couple of days of work. Can you imagine what she'd do to me if I went over her head to the CEO?"

I shudder at the very thought of it. "I already had to fend her off earlier this week after she saw pictures of me at the party."

"Oh?" asks Jonah.

"She saw me mingling with a bunch of business people and CEOs, and had her PA call and order me to find some new clients for the company."

"I thought you were her PA?" says Jonah, looking a little confused.

"Sarah is her permanent PA," I say. "I'm more of a chew toy."

Jonah laughs and looks at me with one brow raised. "So, you aren't going to try and network with me?"

"No," I say. "I told her you were a friend of a friend. Which is technically true."

Jonah doesn't answer. There's a flash of something across his face, and once again I assume he's about to switch into moody mode and disappear for the night. To my surprise, he throws the towel down on the counter and takes a step toward me.

"Do you have a room in mind?" he asks.

"Hmm?" I ask, an expression of pure innocence on my face. I know exactly what he's asking me, but I've been pushing it to the back of my mind all day—assuming that he wasn't serious, or that the power would be back on, or that Jonah's seaplane would magically drift back to the island.

"Well, there are a lot of them to get through," he says, taking another step forward. He reaches down and laces his finger through mine, then lifts my hand right up over my head, stretching me out and causing my hips to bay forward. "We really do need to get started."

"I didn't... I mean. I haven't showered since... last night," I say.

"Me neither," he croons, leaning down and kissing my throat.

I suck in a gasp. "I stink."

"I only have myself to blame," he says, running his tongue up my neck to my earlobe.

I have no more resistance left in me. "Kitchen?" I offer weakly, my voice trembling, and Jonah covers my mouth with his and kisses me deeply.

Chapter 12

I wake feeling fully rested but slightly annoyed. There's a loud, metallic clanking sound coming from outside, repeating itself every few seconds; it must have been irritating me even in my sleep. I roll over in the bed and see only creased sheets where Jonah used to be.

I get dressed and head outside to find him. He's in a small shed just outside the main compound, wearing shorts and sliders, and banging a wrench of some description against a metal nut.

"Still nothing?" I ask.

"Oh, hey, Franchesca," he says.

It doesn't even irritate me anymore to hear my full name. I anticipate the extra syllables now and enjoy the sound of them rolling off his tongue.

"I'm trying to loosen this nut to get inside and see if there's any water in here from the storm," he says, banging at the nut again. "Could explain why the power's still out."

I figure the contraption he's pointing his wrench at is some sort of generator. The room we're in is pretty sparse, and I have no idea what any of this stuff does, but all the wires I can see are neatly tied and there doesn't seem to be any damage. I lean back against the wall, but my shoulder blade hits something sharp and I turn around to see what it is.

There's a small box on the wall with a single switch in it. The button is green, but a small label next to it says "OFF".

"The satellites and receivers look fine, so if I can get this heap of junk working we should be back in b——"

I flick the switch upward, and the big box that Jonah was banging immediately whirrs to life. There's a loud beep, and Jonah looks over at me in astonishment. His gaze moves to my hand, and then to the switch it's resting on it, then back to my face, and his shoulders slump.

"Power!" I say, delighted.

"My ego!" groans Jonah, clutching his chest and screwing up his face as though he's having a heart attack.

I laugh at him. "Don't worry, your secret is safe with me."

"It better be," he says. "If Matt found out about this, I'd never hear the end of it."

I lift my fingers to my lips and mime closing them with an invisible zipper.

"Right," he says, tossing the wrench onto the floor. "Let's go see if we have comms again, and maybe we can get you to the ball on time."

Part of me is delighted that we're up and running and that I'll at least be able to email the office and let them know what's going on. Another part of me is despondent, knowing that I'm one step closer to the end of my time on this island with Jonah.

I know, I know. All I wanted was a fling, and he doesn't date, and I don't have time to date. But things have just been so comfortable between us since the bunker, and he's frankly an *incredible* lover. I have no idea how I'm supposed to stand in the same room as him at Matt and Robbie's parties in the future, and *not* think about the time he made me stand on the bed with my panties around my knees just so he could admire me. Even now, I can barely think about it without feeling a twitch between my legs.

I follow Jonah into the house, check my emails quickly, and fire one off to Sarah to explain the situation—and also tell her not to mention anything to Jessica unless I don't show up on Monday morning.

"Well, that's useful," Jonah mutters from behind his laptop on the opposite side of the table.

"What?" I ask.

"Matt sent me an email to let me know there was a nasty storm blowing in. They had to alter course to avoid it, apparently."

"When did he send it?" I ask.

"Just after my meeting with Hong Kong," he says.

"So does anyone know we're stuck here?"

"Yes," he says. "Matt's pilot is on his way with my driver, Greg. There's no runway on this island, so they'll have to fly to a bigger one further South and then hire a boat to come get us."

"What's a driver going to do?" I ask, remembering my conversation with Eric at the party. "There aren't any roads here."

"That's just his job title," he says. "He's really sort of a driver, assistant, bodyguard type of thing."

"Oh," I say.

"They're on their way already. They should be here by this evening."

"Oh," I say again, hearing my voice come out a little flatter.

A long moment of silence passes between us. Jonah stares out of the window and then back down at his laptop screen, while I scroll through my phone and try to ignore the sinking feeling in my gut. I feel like some kind of reverse Dorothy, being forced to go back to Kansas even though what I really want is to stay in Oz.

"Shower?" Jonah asks abruptly, pushing his laptop screen down and getting to his feet.

"Huh?" I ask.

"Do you want to take a shower with me?" he asks. "The water will be hot by now."

"Yes," I say without hesitation. "Yes, I want to do that." I toss my phone onto the table and practically jump out of my chair. I will drown my worries in soapy suds, all over Jonah's body. And I will finally achieve the ambition I told Robbie about all those months ago, just after I met Jonah for the very first time; I will slide down him like a fire station pole.

∽

Sadly, but very predictably given who they work for, Greg and Matt's pilot, Jay, do indeed arrive that evening, right on time.

They're both pleasant guys. The boat they've hired to take us home is much smaller than the yacht I arrived on, and as it glides and skips along the water as the island gets smaller and smaller behind us, I feel a sinking feeling in my stomach.

The easy intimacy that Jonah and I shared for the last few days has slipped back into a more formal "our best friends are married to each other" vibe, now that we have company. I'm not sure if that's my doing or his, but I suspect a little of both.

We arrive at the airstrip a short time later and walk straight off the boat onto the waiting plane. I distract myself with my phone during the flight home, catching up on emails and texting Robbie. She was frantic at first, when she found out what had happened and couldn't get in contact with me, but now that she knows I'm OK she's shifted to gently probing about the couple of days I spent alone on the island with Jonah.

I would never normally keep anything from her—especially gossip about a hot fling—but I find myself deflecting her questions and implying, without outright lying, that nothing happened. There's something about the last few days that was different than all the flings that came before. Something I want to hold onto just for me, to remember in my own way.

I feel the plane start to descend, and I glance up from my phone. Jonah is in a seat a little further down the plane. He has his laptop open in front of him, but he's not looking at it. He's looking at me.

I smile at him, and he smiles back, his lips closed. An unspoken, bittersweet emotion passes quietly between us; something like… a pleasant resignation. The realization that the last few days have been wonderful, and that we could have been great together, somehow and somewhere. Maybe between two different versions of ourselves, in a different world. But not us, and not here, and not now.

A few moments later, we touch down in New York. This is my stop; Jonah is traveling onwards to Chicago. I stand up and pull my carry-on out of the overhead compartment, then turn around and give Jonah a little wave. He raises his hand and waves back. I think I see his jaw tremble slightly, but it could be my imagination. And that's it; our last interaction, the end of our fairytale vacation romance. I step off the plane and back into reality.

Well, *almost* back into reality; given who's paying for this trip, I naturally have a limousine waiting at the airfield to take me home. Greg pulls my remaining bags out of the plane's cargo hold and hefts them into the trunk. I climb into the back and Greg climbs into the driver's seat. I suddenly realize that I'm not sure of the etiquette here. Is it like, taxi rules?

"Um…" I begin, "I live at…"

Greg shoots me a friendly smile in the mirror. "It's okay, ma'am. I already have all the details. We'll have you home in no time."

I smile and sit back. One last time that Jonah has taken care of me. It's getting late and I'm feeling a little jet-lagged, so I'm glad of Jonah's consideration, but for some reason, I feel an unexpected pang of melancholy at the gesture.

The drive home, in this car, is like drifting on air. We arrive at my apartment block just before midnight. The elevator is broken—I can barely remember when it last worked—so Greg lugs my cases up the stairs for me, and has the good grace not to comment on the size of my apartment, or linger too long after dropping my luggage inside.

I'm too exhausted to unpack but too wired to sleep, so I make sure my alarm is set for the morning, put on a slow jazz playlist that reminds me of Jonah, and make myself some cocoa. Sitting in the dim light of my apartment, I think back over everything that's happened, squeezing the last morsels of enjoyment from the amazing adventure I've just been on before I have to face the music tomorrow.

Chapter 13

"Well? Did you get any info on Sullivan Wells?"

I look up from my computer with a start. Jessica is striding towards my desk, somehow looming over me despite still being ten feet away. Sarah scampers around the corner after her, looking her usual flustered Monday morning self.

"Uh," I say, willing my mind to kick into gear despite the lack of sleep. "No. I wasn't with those people anymore by the time Sarah called me."

I glance at Sarah—it's really more of a glare—and she mouths *sorry* back to me.

"Why were they with you, anyway?" asks Jessica, coming to a stop in front of my desk and narrowing her eyes suspiciously.

Note the way she asks the question. Not *how do I know them*. Not *why was I with them*. No. She wants to know why *they* deigned to spend their time with *me*, a country creature from another world.

"They're friends of a friend," I say.

She raises one brow and eyeballs me even harder.

"Of a friend," I add for good measure.

"Mmm," she says, looking me up and down. "Well, if you get an opportunity like that again, make the most of it."

"Right," I say, nodding. Anything to get her away from my desk so I can finish my first coffee of the day in peace. "I will. Thanks for the advice."

Jessica gives me a single nod and heads into her office.

"I'm so sorry," says Sarah in an urgent whisper. "I was going to tell her you were just at a party with those CEOs, but then Tony from Compliance finally brought the sales reports back and there was an anomaly and... well. You know what she's like. That was the only thing that mattered to her for the rest of the week, and she wasn't interested in hearing anything from me."

"Don't sweat it," I say, picking up my coffee and blowing across the top of it. I'm desperately in need of the caffeine, but when Sarah doesn't move I lower my cup again and look up at her.

"Did you get my books?" she asks expectantly.

I'd completely forgotten about them until right this second.

"Robbie's on vacation for a few weeks," I tell her. "But I'll chase them up for you as soon as she's back, okay?"

"Thanks," says Sarah with a delighted smile. She practically floats out of the room, and I finally get a chance to sip my coffee.

I close my eyes, letting the bitter taste flow over my tongue and around it, willing some of the caffeine to absorb sublingually and grant me a shred of energy. I swallow and sigh, breathing out slowly and trying to force some of the lingering melancholy about Jonah out with it. I open my eyes slowly... and Jessica is standing *right there* in front of me.

"Jesus!" I hiss, almost jumping out of my skin. I swear, sometimes I think this woman can teleport. Some coffee sloshes over the side of my cup and drips onto my desk, and I quickly grab some tissues to mop up the mess.

Jessica looks at me, palpably unimpressed.

"Go through these," she says, dropping a thick, heavy file onto my desk. "And see if you can spot the anomalies Tony found last week. I want to know what happened and why. Get me a risk report and recommendations by..." she glances at the calendar on the wall. "I'm in a generous mood, so I'll give you two weeks."

I drop the soiled tissues into the waste basket beside my desk and reach for the file, trying not to look too surprised at the fact that she's giving me some actual accounting work to do.

"Sure," I say. "I can do that."

I'm pretty sure she's only giving me this because she's seen me socializing with a bunch of what she regards as "worthy" people, but I'll take what I can get. I'll work on it every evening and knock it out of the park, and maybe she'll give me more, and I'll get to do something other than waste away in the copy room for the next eight months.

"Don't fail," she says. I think this is as close to a pep talk as she's capable of.

"Right," I say, clutching the file to my chest.

As soon as she's gone, I open the file and pick my way through it, combing over line after line of financial records, trying to spot anomalies. I'm so tired that I know I'll end up having to go back over these pages again later, but at least I finally feel like I'm doing something that will matter to somebody at some point. Even if it's only Tony in Compliance.

After lunch, just as I'm settling in with the folder again, my phone buzzes.

Unknown Number
Dinner Thursday?

I frown at the screen, trying to figure out who would be inviting me to dinner on Thursday. Is it someone from a dating app whose number I forgot to save? Or worse— someone from a dating app whose number I intentionally deleted?

I'm too tired to have any patience, so I just tap out the obvious question.

Me
Who's this?

Unknown Number

```
Jonah. In town for deal.
```

My heart skips several beats. Luckily, I also start breathing like someone who's just come up after ten minutes underwater, otherwise, I might actually think I was dead.

"Are you okay?"

I look across the room to Sarah, who's staring at me with a look of alarm on her face. Jesus, is it that obvious? Am I hyperventilating?

"Yeah," I say, consciously slowing my breathing. "Yeah, I'm fine. Just… found a double entry."

She screws up her face. "O-kaaay," she says slowly and looks back down at her tablet.

Absolutely nailed that one, Fran. Now your closest co-worker thinks you have a strange and possibly intimate relationship with balance sheets.

"Back in a sec," I say quickly, and head for the most sacred of corporate spaces for anyone wanting to conduct private affairs; the ladies' bathroom.

I save Jonah's number to my phone and tap out a reply.

```
                                         Me
                              So like a date?
```

```
Jonah
I don't date.
```

I don't know why, but his response makes me smile. I immediately think about the risk report Jessica wants from me. Usually, I'd spend every waking moment on it until it was done, but I manage to convince myself that one night off won't do any harm. It might even be good for me to take a breather and clear my head.

Me
Sure, I'll go on a not-date with you.

Jonah
Pick you up at 7. Where?

Me
My place. What should I wear?

Jonah
Clothes.

Me
What sort of clothes?

Jonah
Yours, I'd assume.

I glare at the door of the stall, my lips pressed together.

Me
I mean formal or casual???

Jonah
Wear the yellow dress you wore to the
party. See you Thurs @ 7.

I guess that's something else I can add to my ever-growing encyclopedia of Jonah; the way he trailed his eyes up and down my body at the party meant he liked what I was wearing. I file it beside "he swallows hard when he's getting horny."

∼

Time is weird for the next few days. It goes way too quickly, considering the amount of work I have to do—naturally, Jessica has not reduced any of my other responsibilities to let me work on the risk report—and yet it also seems to be moving painfully slow every time I think about seeing Jonah again.

He hasn't contacted me since he asked me to dinner, so I take it on faith that he'll be on time to pick me up. When Thursday finally rolls around, Jessica is out of the office for a meeting about some fundraiser she's organizing, so I manage to leave a little early and drop into the dry cleaners to pick up my dress on the way home.

There's a knock on my door at exactly 7 pm, and it immediately sends a rush of panic through me. I had assumed that Jonah would text me from outside rather than coming up here himself—the place is a complete mess after I've spent the last couple of hours getting ready. I grab some hair-covered wax strips from the table and throw them in the trash, kick my hairdryer under the couch, and open the door.

Jonah is standing outside, wearing business slacks and a white shirt with the sleeves rolled up and the top couple of buttons undone. He looks amazing.

"Hey," I say, slipping out into the hall and pulling the door closed behind me as quickly as I can. I really hope he didn't catch a glimpse of the mess. Or the size of it. Or the mold patch on the wall above the single, tiny window.

I needn't have worried. Jonah trails his gaze slowly to my feet and back up, and smiles when he meets my eyes.

"Hey. I like this dress," he says, and leans in, planting a gentle kiss on the side of my neck.

A ripple of pleasure rolls from the point where his lips meet my neck down my spine. It's the single most "we're definitely going on a date" greeting I've ever experienced, but I decide that's better left unsaid.

"Thanks," I say, turning around to lock the door so he doesn't see the slight flush on my cheeks. "You look very *straight outta the boardroom*. How did the deal go?"

"Fine," he says, gesturing for me to go ahead of him. "We got it done. How's your awful boss?"

"Still awful," I say, starting down the stairs.

Greg is waiting just outside, and he pulls the limousine door open as we exit the building. The last time I saw him, he was wearing cargo shorts and a polo shirt. This time, he's all dressed up in a full chauffeur uniform, complete with hat.

"Good evening, Ms. Potts," he says, very formally.

"Hi, Greg," I say, grinning at him. I duck into the limo and slide across the seat, and Jonah takes the seat directly opposite me. Naturally, I start over-analyzing his choice of seat, but I force myself to stop when I notice him looking at me.

"I won't pour drinks," he says when I make eye contact. "The restaurant isn't that far. Unless you want one?"

"No, no," I say. "I'm good, thanks. Where are we going?"

I know for a fact that there are no billionaire-level restaurants in my part of town.

"This little Italian place I know. It's small and a bit out-of-the-way, but the food is amazing."

"Huh," I say, unable to keep the surprise out of my voice.

"What?" he asks.

"Nothing. I just figured you might prefer Michelin stars and fancy sommeliers and all."

He smiles back at me. "Michelin stars and fancy sommeliers have their place. But I don't like it when I bump into
people who end up wanting to talk business with me. And
besides, finding amazing little places to eat that are off the
beaten track is one of my favorite things to do."

"Oh my God," I say. "Me, too! I love that. When you
wander around until someplace just has an atmosphere
that sucks you in?"

"Yeah," Jonah agrees, grinning at my enthusiasm. "Little
places where the chef is missing a finger and the tables
wobble."

"Yes!" I laugh.

The smile on his face is easy and relaxed as he sits there,
watching me. I don't know why I'm so surprised that he
likes finding restaurants the same way I do. Nothing about
him has given me the impression that he's a snob. And
everything about him has shown me that he adores food
and wine. And whisky.

"Here we are," he says, as the car pulls up.

Greg opens the door and Jonah steps out first. He turns
around to take my hand and guides me out of the car.

"We'll be a couple of hours," Jonah tells Greg. "I'll call
you."

Greg gives him a single nod in response. Jonah offers me
his arm and I slip my fingers into the crook of his elbow,
feeling very much like I might be on a date.

～

The restaurant is gorgeous, full of small, round tables
draped with gingham cloths and surrounded by rickety

wooden chairs. The lighting is warm, dimmed just enough so that the candles flickering on each table add to the ambiance. Sizzling sounds and savory scents emanate from an open kitchen, and the place is absolutely packed, the way that small places that locals love always are.

"Hey, Tommaso," says Jonah as the greeter comes over.

The man has gray hair that's slicked back, and he's wearing a white t-shirt and black pants, with a red apron tied around his waist. He has a kind smile on a weathered face that could be anything from fifty to seventy years old, and when he speaks he does so with a strong, New York Italian accent.

"Mr. Wells! It's been a minute, eh? And you have a beautiful lady with you. Ciao bella," says the man, taking my hand and kissing the back of it.

"This is Franchesca," says Jonah. "Franchesca, this is Tommaso. His family has owned this place for... what?" he asks, looking back at Tommaso. "Seventy years?"

"Sixty-eight," says Tommaso, grinning at me. "You know, my great-grandmother was named Franchesca?" He grabs a couple of menus from beside the small podium near the door and doesn't wait for me to respond.

"I saved your favorite table, Mr. Wells. If you don't mind... I have a new server. She's a little nervous to be working such a busy night, but it's been hard to get staff. You know how it goes, being a businessman yourself and all."

"Sure do," says Jonah, as he stands aside for me to go ahead of him and squeeze between two tables.

"But being a regular, maybe you wouldn't mind if she serves your table, eh?"

"No problem," says Jonah. "If it's okay with you?"

It takes me a second to realize he's talking to me.

"Oh, sure," I say, nodding. "Of course. I used to be a server, myself. We all have to learn somehow, right?"

"Right," says Tommaso, looking delighted. He pulls a chair out for me to take a seat, while Jonah seats himself. "I'll send her along in a moment."

"Lovely place," I tell Jonah, as Tommaso weaves his way back through the tables.

"Wait 'til you taste the food," he says.

"Can't wait," I say. We both fall silent to look over the menus until a thought pops into my head.

"Hey, did you ever get your plane back?"

"Yeah," says Jonah. "It washed up a few days later and a couple of islands over, so I had someone tow it back to our island. It's in the garage near the house until I can get someone out there to check it over."

"Well, that was lucky, though, right? It could have been out there just floating in the Atlantic fore—"

"H-hi."

The voice that interrupts me is so quiet I almost miss it. I look up to find a girl standing beside our table, wearing a nervous smile and hunching over a tiny notepad with a pen gripped so tight in her fingers that her skin is turning white around it. She can't be more than eighteen, if that.

"Hey," says Jonah.

"I'm Ah-uh, Ava," she says. "I'll be your server tonight. Can I take your order?"

We both order, and I'm struck by how kind Jonah is. He takes his time, never speaking while she's writing, and he points to the items he wants on the menu whenever she seems to struggle. I do the same, and our pre-meal drinks arrive in fairly short order.

"Oh, by the way—you need to send me your bank details," says Jonah. "So I can pay you for the motorcycle."

"I can't just give out my bank details!" I exclaim, in mock outrage. "How do I know I can trust you? What if you're a scammer?"

"You got me," he says. "Matt and I actually made all of our money by running elaborate games on a private island, promising big prizes to unsuspecting young women, and then emptying out their bank accounts."

I manage not to laugh. Instead, I play along. "Is Robbie a mark?" I gasp.

"Definitely," says Jonah, nodding. "She'll wake up in sixty years and Matt will have taken off with her savings. It's just how we roll."

"Wow," I say, shaking my head. I can't help grinning at this point. "What do you even call a male honeypot? A gigolo, I guess? Is that what you two are?"

"Uh… hi?"

The server is back and looking slightly alarmed at the part of our conversation she overheard. She manages—barely—to get our dishes onto the table without dropping them, though her hands shake the whole time.

The food really is amazing. My bruschetta appetizer is bursting with fresh flavor, the tomato sauce on my entree is the most tomatoey-tasting thing I've ever put in my mouth,

179

and the pasta is perfectly al dente. And the wine that Tommaso insisted on choosing for us is so smooth it feels like I'm drinking velvet. Who needs a Michelin-star sommelier when you can have the sixty-year-old Italian owner of a hole-in-the-wall family restaurant?

Once we're done with our food, Ava clears away our plates and brings us the dessert menus. I'm poring over mine, trying to decide between tiramisu and sbrisolona, when Jonah clears his throat.

"So, are you going to stay at my place?"

I feel my pulse pick up instantly but try not to show it.

"No pressure if you don't want to," he adds.

"Don't you live in Chicago?" I ask, stalling for time. "It's a bit far to travel to work in the morning."

"I have an apartment a few blocks away," he says. "For when I come here on business."

I still can't answer. The thought of spending another night with Jonah, of letting him do all the things he did to me on the island, is thrilling. But I also know me. Well enough to know that, outside of weddings and vacations, I'm not the sort of woman who can just do a fling. I'll fall. And I'll fall hard. And that will end when Jonah inevitably walks away to go about his fantastical billionaire life, leaving me on the floor, heartbroken and surrounded by the tattered remnants of my dreams. I might even lose my mojo at work and miss out on the real internship I'm chasing. I'd love to be a fling girl. I'm just not.

"Oh my God!"

I look up and see Ava standing beside our table, her eyes wide with shock. She's only there for a moment before she suddenly darts off towards the kitchen. As I pull myself out of my thoughts, I gradually become aware of a strange smell and feel an odd heat against my cheek. I turn my head slightly towards where it feels like it's coming from, and suddenly everything makes sense.

The heat and the smell are coming from the menu I'm holding, which is now on fire because I held it too close to the candle for too long while I was lost in my own thoughts. And I guess Jonah was pretty fixated on me as well because he looks as surprised as I do.

Thinking quickly, I fold the menu, ready to carefully dunk it into the jug of water on the table. I'm actually quite pleased with myself for coming up with a solution so fast, before this escalates into a *real* social faux-pas, which would be just typical of my luck. But just then, I see a flash of movement out of the corner of my eye. Ava is dashing back towards us from the kitchen. She's kind of swaying as she runs, and from the glimpses I catch between the tables, I can tell that she's carrying something pretty big with her. As she emerges from the nearest cluster of tables, I finally see what it is.

Oh my God, I think to myself. *She can't possibly be about to-*

FFFFSSHHHHHHHHHHHHHHHHTTTTTTTTTTTT!

My vision whites out and my breath catches in my throat as Ava wildly sprays the wet, foamy contents of the fire extinguisher all over the menu, the candles, the table—and yes, me, covering me from head to midriff in flame-retardant goop.

It's over almost as quickly as it started, and as the hiss of the fire extinguisher dies down, a deathly quiet descends over the entire restaurant, until the only sound to be heard is the traditional Italian music wafting softly in the background.

I reach up slowly and scoop away the layer of frothy goop covering my eyes. Ava is standing in front of the table, the hose still pointed at me, trembling from head to toe. Every other customer in the restaurant is staring over at us, mouths agape—I see one guy who is *still holding his fork in the air halfway to his mouth*, having apparently stopped mid-bite to look at me with a dumbfounded expression on his face. I look over at Jonah, who has escaped almost completely unscathed aside from a few small flecks on his suit jacket, and his face is aghast—though looking closer, I almost think I see him struggling to keep in a laugh. He bolts out of his chair and comes over to kneel beside me.

"Are you alright?" he asks, quietly.

"*Ava! What the hell are you doin'?*" Tommaso practically screams as he runs over to us.

"I'm sorry!" cries Ava, sounding like she's on the verge of tears. "I'm sorry! The training video said that fire is the most dangerous thing that can happen!"

Tommaso looks at her like she's insane. "*In the kitchen!* A fire *in the kitchen* is an emergency, not when someone burns a menu! That happens every other night! There are candles on *every table*, for God's sake!"

I'm still sitting in my seat, too shocked to say anything, taking in the bizarre tableau before me. Jonah is kneeling attentively in front of me, dabbing gently at the goop on my face with a napkin. Behind him, Ava has her hand over her mouth, shaking as she tries to stop herself from bursting into tears, and Tommaso looks like he's mentally working out how much he can sell the place for when the DOH shuts him down—if Yelp doesn't get him first.

Beyond them are a sea of faces, all turned towards me, their expressions frozen in various stages of shock, disbelief, and confusion.

Logically, I know this should be a humiliating situation to find myself in. But the scene before me is so bizarre, so patently ridiculous, that I somehow find myself transcending the bounds of embarrassment. It's as though my brain has overloaded, like there's no room for it to feel mortified because it's too busy processing the absurdity. After what feels like a very long time, it finally manages to come up with a single thought: *Well, this really is just your luck.*

I can't help myself. I snort a laugh.

I didn't think it was possible for the people in this room to look *more* shocked, but somehow they manage it. Jonah raises his eyebrows, and for a moment looks genuinely concerned that I've gone off the deep end. But I've started, and now I can't stop. The snort turns into a proper laugh and then, as the absurdity of the situation seeps further and further into my mind, I dissolve into a fit of giggles.

Jonah's mouth wavers, and he chuckles. My suspicions from earlier seem to be right because he looks genuinely relieved at not having to stop himself from laughing anymore. He breaks into a series of guffaws, and before long we're both laughing our asses off.

Our laughter seems to break the tension across the whole restaurant, and soon everyone is laughing along with us. I see a lot of people raise their glasses towards me and give me a big smile and nod as if to say, "Good for you!" Ava is cry-laughing through tear-stained eyes, and Tomasso is shaking his head, a relieved grin on his face.

"Gino!" he calls to one of the servers. "Get this lady a towel."

The server reappears with a couple of towels in short order, and Jonah takes them from him. He hunkers down beside me again and starts wiping the remaining foam from my face and arms, still chuckling to himself, while I scoop handfuls of it from my dress.

"I'll tell you one thing, Franchesca Potts," says Jonah, smiling broadly at me, "You're not boring."

I'm not sure if he can see me blush under the foam concealer, but it's there.

"You want to get out of here?"

"That would be good," I say, smiling back at him. "I appreciate your towel work, but I think I'm gonna need a long shower to get rid of all this. I guess I just don't have much luck with birds."

Jonah looks perplexed.

"Ava," I say. "It means bird, right? And the goose at the wedding…"

He laughs. "That doesn't bode well," he says. "My name literally means 'dove.'"

"Well, in that case, I guess I'll just have to stay on my guard around you," I reply, shooting him the most coquettish look I can manage while still half-covered in fire extinguisher foam.

He gives me a wicked grin in return and stands up to tap something out on his phone. Within seconds, Greg is standing beside the table.

"Boss," he says, handing Jonah a folded cloth.

When Jonah shakes it out, I can see that it's a suit jacket—most likely the one Jonah was wearing to his meeting earlier. He offers me his hand, helps me to my feet, and slips the jacket around my shoulders.

"Ready to go?" he asks.

"Yes," I say, looking mournfully down at the foam-covered table, and the little blackened edge of the dessert menu sticking up in the middle. I grab my purse and flick some foam off the side of it. "But you owe me a dessert."

"Hold me to it," says Jonah, dropping a wad of cash onto the table.

"Hey," I say. "Wait." I start rummaging in my purse. "I need to pay half."

"It's done," he says.

"No, it's not," I tell him, pulling out my wallet. "I can pay half. I just sold a motorcycle, you know."

"Franchesca, it's f—"

"It's important to me," I cut in. I watch his mouth form an irritated line, and I can almost hear his brain ticking back over all the times I've told him how much I hate it when Robbie tries to give me money.

"Besides," I continue, "if you pay for dinner, then this really *is* a date. Officially. And as everyone knows," I put on a deep caveman-like voice, "*Jonah no date.*"

His eyes sparkle slightly, and his mouth curls into an almost imperceptible smile. "Okay," he concedes.

"If I may," says a voice, and Tomasso appears beside us again. Ava is peeking out from behind him, barely able to

185

make eye contact. "This conversation is moot, because your meal this evening is, of course, on the house."

"I'm really, really sorry I ruined your evening," squeaks Ava, her voice cracking.

"Oh honey, don't worry about it," I say, putting my now relatively-clean hands on her shoulders reassuringly. "If it wasn't for you, this would've just been a fantastic meal. Now it's a fantastic meal *and* a story I'll be telling my grandkids about!"

She cry-laughs again and then wraps her arms around me in a hug. Tomasso looks at me appreciatively.

"Beautiful *and* gracious!" he grins to Jonah. "This one, she's a keeper, Mr. Wells."

"Don't give her any ideas!" Jonah grins, wagging his finger at Tomasso as we head for the exit.

∾

Greg opens the car for us when we get outside, and we take the same seats we had earlier; me on the back seat, facing forward, Jonah opposite me. The window behind him slides down and I see Greg's eyes in the rearview.

"Where to, Boss?" asks Greg.

Jonah fixes me with a questioning stare.

I'd almost forgotten the question he asked me over dinner, before all hell broke loose. Now it's back, looming larger than ever, as though it's sitting right there in the car between us.

"I have to get to work in the morning," I say.

"Greg will drive you," says Jonah.

I glance at Greg in the rearview again, but he just stares placidly back at me.

"I don't have any clothes for work."

"Greg will get you some," says Jonah.

"I don't have anything to sleep in," I say.

"You won't be sleeping much, Franchesca."

There's a little click and a quiet whirr as Greg, apparently having decided the conversation has become more intimate than he needs to hear, slides the window back up.

I wonder if he does this often. How many of Jonah's one-night stands have been in the back of this limo, powerless to resist his charms? How many one-night stands *have* there been, for that matter? Or multiple-night stands? Not many, according to him, but how would I really know? And do I really care?

"Okay."

Apparently, I do not care.

"Okay?" Jonah says.

"Yes," I say. "Okay."

"You're sure, Franchesca?" he says. "Because I want you to be sure. I'm just telling you that the obstacles you think are in your way, aren't really obstacles at all."

Well, if I wasn't sure before, I am now that he said my name. It's so strange, how a name I've disliked for most of my life can suddenly sound like honey in my ears. Every time he says it, I feel a little flutter in the pit of my stomach.

"I'm sure," I say. "I would like to end our not-date with some not-sex."

A brief flash of hesitation passes across Jonah's face. It's barely there a split second before he covers it with a smirk —if I weren't looking directly at him, I would have missed it.

He hits a button beside him to bring the partition window down again.

"My place, please, Greg," he says, and we pull out onto the road.

Chapter 14

I wake up serenely the next morning in Jonah's luxurious super king bed, stretching lazily beneath the Egyptian cotton sheets, like a cat basking in the morning sun. My phone's alarm is thrumming gently on the bedside table, but I'm surprised to find I don't need it; I'm already awake and feeling more rested than I have in a long time. I can hear some distant clanking and banging, and then as the rest of my senses catch up to me, I smell the wonderful aroma of bacon and coffee drifting through the apartment. My stomach growls.

Jonah has left one of his shirts on the bed for me since my dress from last night is still covered in the powdery remnants of the fire extinguisher foam. I slip the shirt on, button it up to the middle of my chest, throw my hair up into a messy bun, and head out to find him.

He's standing in the kitchen looking like an Adonis. It's not every man who can pull off sweats and a plain white t-shirt, but he definitely manages it. Probably something to do with the fact that his enormous pecs are stretching the t-shirt taught.

"Hey," he says as I walk in, and I reluctantly tear my gaze away from his chest. He pauses where he is, with a spatula still in his hand, and runs his gaze from my face down to my bare feet and back up. Fair's fair, I suppose.

"Hey," I say. "You must've been up early."

"I like to get in a workout before I start the day," he says. "And since you're working today and I'm not, I figured I'd make sure you're fed."

This all feels very domestic. Which is fine by me, but I'm a little surprised Jonah hasn't jumped out the window to escape.

"You've worked out already?" I ask, looking at him like he's crazy. I pick my phone up and look at the screen, just to be sure I didn't get the time wrong. Nope. It's just after 6 am. I set my alarm early last night to make sure I'd be able to get to work on time from Jonah's apartment since I'm not *entirely* sure where in the city I am.

"Not much," he says. "Just a run on the treadmill. I got up at about five."

"Do you always get up that early?" I ask, regarding him the way you might regard a particularly interesting zoo specimen.

"Not always," he says. "I slept in on the island, didn't I?"

"Okay, but as a rule…"

"As a rule, I'm usually up before six."

"Fascinating," I say. I'd never rise before midday if I had the choice.

"Have a seat," says Jonah with a grin, directing me to the dining table on the far side of the cavernous space he calls a living room. "How do you like your bacon and eggs?"

"Crispy, please," I say. "And over easy."

"Coffee?"

"I'll take a little cream if you have it?"

The table's been set for two, with a glass of freshly-squeezed orange juice already in front of each. I pick one up and sip it.

It's an amazing view. I can see half of Central Park and the beginnings of the morning traffic. A few people are already out on the streets—mostly city workers, but I can also see some harried-looking businesspeople in suits striding down the sidewalks on their way to their offices. I stare at them in much the same way I did when Jonah told me he gets up at 5am, and I decide to name this particular species of people "Jessicas."

I watch the world move underneath me, fascinated, thinking how it seems as faraway and inconsequential from this lofty perch as ants scurrying along the tunnels in their nests, until Jonah places the plate down in front of me.

"Thanks," I say.

"Any time," he says, sitting opposite me. "I got a call from Matt this morning. Business stuff, mostly, but he said he'll deliver the motorcycle directly to me. So I've wired your money."

This is bittersweet news. It means I'll have more money, which is great, but it also means that I no longer have a pretext to contact Jonah in the future. And yes, I *had* imagined him coming to pick up his bike from my apartment, and riding me off into the sunset.

On the bike, I mean. And then later yes, the other way as well.

"Awesome," I say with a smile. Mustn't be ungrateful. "Thanks!"

"Thank *you*," he says. "I have an amazing new Harley."

I eat my breakfast quickly, and it tastes divine. Something about all the "exercise" I got last night, after the shock of being publicly turned into a human meringue, has given me an appetite. We chat amiably through the meal until Jonah pauses for a moment and clears his throat.

"So I have to go to a thing in Chicago in a few weeks," he begins.

"Oh?" I say.

"It's nothing important, but I have to make an appearance because I was invited by someone I want to do a deal with."

"Okaaaay," I say, wondering why he's telling me.

"I have a plus one."

"Oh!" I say, surprised but not at all displeased. "Another not-date?"

"Sure," he says with a grin. "Or a date, if you want."

Oh. Well, that's something new. And he's not backing away, or wearing an expression that looks like he's about to bolt out the door at any second. He's pretty calm, actually.

"Well," I say, thoughtfully, "I'd actually become quite fond of not-dating you. But I suppose I could try a date, just to see if it's any good. What should I wear?"

"Why is that always the first thing you ask?" he says, but his eyes are sparkling.

"Because I'm a poor intern with two good dresses, and one of them is currently covered in fire-retardant powder."

"I'll send you something," he says.

"What something?"

"I don't know," he says. "A dress. I'll find out what the dress code is and send you something."

I open my mouth to speak, but he cuts me off.

"If you're about to protest, save it. This isn't me giving you a handout or whatever other nonsense you're thinking right now. I'm buying you a dress because I like the way you look in them, and I like peeling them off you afterward."

I close my mouth, press my lips together, and then sigh.

"Fine," I say. "As long as it's not a handout, and you're only buying me a dress so you can objectify me, I can live with that."

He grins at me, shakes his head in mock exasperation, and pops the last of his breakfast into his mouth.

～

"That's a new suit."

I'm barely in the office for ten seconds and Jessica is already in front of my desk, looking me over from head to toe.

What she actually means is that this is a much better work outfit than what I normally wear. My usual wardrobe is made up of the best pieces I can thrift from three seasons ago, combined with some basic workwear from Target and Zara. So when Greg arrived this morning with this top-of-the-line designer suit for me to wear, I almost had a heart attack.

And then I got a little weird about it, especially after just agreeing to let Jonah buy me a dress, and I absolutely refused to accept it until Jonah told me that the designer boutique it came from didn't do returns—no exceptions. Which I think was a lie, but by then I was running late.

"Yes, it is," I say to Jessica.

"It suits you," she replies, and my jaw nearly hits the floor.

I mean, it's an amazing suit. It's beautifully cut and it fits so well you'd easily think it was tailored for me. But even so— a compliment from Jessica?

'Thanks?" I say, somehow managing to accidentally inflect it as a question in my shock.

"How's the report coming along?"

"Great," I lie. "Yeah, really good." I should probably have declined Jonah's offer of a date in a few weeks' time, given that it will roughly coincide with the due date for the report, but I'm sure I'll find a way to get it all done.

Her gaze lingers for a moment like she's trying to decide whether to believe me.

"Good," she says at last. "Send Sarah in when she's back."

"Sure thing," I say, and watch her stride off into her office.

As soon as she's gone, I head into the ladies' bathroom and examine my outfit in the mirror, turning this way and that, checking myself out from different angles. There's no denying it—the way I look today, I'd easily pass for a real, honest-to-goodness professional woman.

Chapter 15

The evening before I'm due to fly to Chicago, a delivery driver is waiting for me outside my apartment door when I get home from work. She tells me she has strict instructions to make sure the parcel is handed to me personally, that day. I thank her for waiting, take the box, and head inside.

When I open the package, I have to stifle a gasp. The gown is beautiful. It's made of a shimmering, burnt orange silk with intricate vines and leaves embroidered in gold thread around the bodice. It has a halter neck, a split from the mid-thigh on one side, and it somehow fits me perfectly, as though it's been made from a mold of my figure. The last thing that fit me this well was my bridesmaid dress, and we all know how that turned out.

Jonah's also sent me some matching gold ankle wrap sandals, and a tiny purse just big enough for my phone.

Much as I'm tempted to just wear it all evening and prance about my moldy shoe-box apartment like a princess, I can't. I have to get some work done and finalize this report because otherwise, Jessica is going to wear my entrails for earrings. I hang the gown carefully in my mold-free bedroom and tap out a text to Jonah.

> Me
> Hey, I got the dress. It's beautiful.
> Thank you.

He replies right away, and my heart skips a beat. I've barely heard from him since the night I stayed at his apartment, other than to tell me when and where I'd be picked up.

> Jonah
> You're welcome. See you tomorrow.

Very utilitarian. He's not much of a texter, I've noticed. If he used an emoji I'd probably call Matt and ask him to do a wellness check.

I make myself a cup of lemon and ginger tea and settle in at my small dining table to do a final pass over the report. I've been working on it every night this week and I'm exhausted, but it will be done and I will have met Jessica's brief: "don't fail."

I'm actually pretty impressed with the recommendations I've made. The anomalies ended up being due to the mishandling of a petty cash box in HR. Why is HR still using cash this far into the twenty-first century? No idea. Why does the company insist on communicating their sales reports by passing a single hard copy between departments —again, I remind you, in the third decade of the twenty-first century? Alas, these are questions for after hell year.

By the time I've double- and triple-checked everything, it's 3am. I'm not being picked up until mid-afternoon tomorrow, so I'll at least get *some* sleep. Hopefully, that'll get rid of the stress that's been building up for the last week or two as I've raced to finish the report on time. The promise of a trip to Chicago and the chance to see Jonah again is all that's kept me going.

≈

By the time I get a message to tell me that my driver is outside, I'm ready to roll. Jonah told me that the cabin of the plane he's sending to pick me up is big enough to let me change during the flight, which is a sentence that my economy-class mind can scarcely even comprehend. But I assume he knows what he's talking about, so I've packed my dress carefully into its garment bag, ready for the flight. The driver—not Greg, who will be meeting me after we land—takes the dress and hangs it on a hook in the driver's cabin of the limousine, puts my overnight bag into the trunk, and off we head.

I've heard stories from Robbie, who has done plenty of billionaire-class traveling since she met Matt, but actually being inside a private plane cabin that's bigger than my entire apartment still takes my breath away. There's even a *bathroom,* for crying out loud. Like a fully functional bathroom with a fancy washbasin and vanity counter. Imagine having so much money you can put a plush bathroom in your private plane just in case you need to freshen up mid-flight.

I change into my dress, slip on my shoes, and apply my makeup in the bathroom mirror. There are a few little bumps as we pass through turbulence that nearly turn my cat wings into bat wings, but I manage to get a full face on well before the flight is over. Which gives me plenty of time to start worrying about what kind of event a billionaire attends when he's trying to secure a business deal. Like, who's going to be there? Wealthy sultans? A couple of kings? *The President?*

My stomach is tying itself into nervous knots by the time we land, but I begin to feel a bit better when Greg meets me at the landing pad—which is on top of a skyscraper, naturally—and offers me his hand as I step down from the cabin. He collects my luggage, and we step into an elevator that takes us all the way from the roof of the building to the basement parking lot. I climb into the back of the limo while Greg taps something out on his phone, and a couple of minutes later, Jonah opens the door and slides in beside me.

"You look incredible," he says and leans right in to place a kiss on the side of my neck. If this is what a date is like, I'll take it.

"Thanks," I say. "You look pretty good, yourself."

He's wearing a navy tux and bow tie with a crisp, white shirt. His hair has been trimmed since I last saw him, and that amazing cologne wafts right up my nostrils and takes me back to every time I've been up close with him.

He shrugs, but he has a smug grin on his face. "I try."

He knocks on the window behind him, and Greg sets off. We drive for around twenty minutes, chatting about what we've been up to since the last time we met. Jonah asks me about my report and how it's going, but he has a sort of nervous energy about him that I haven't seen before, and which makes him seem permanently half-distracted.

We finally pull up outside the venue. The door opens and Jonah gets out, but when I look over his shoulder, I can see that it wasn't Greg who opened it. It's someone else, wearing a very different uniform. A valet, maybe?

Jonah turns and offers me his hand. I take it… and emerge into what can only be described as absolute chaos. There are people everywhere, camera flashes in every direction I look, and, I notice with a sinking feeling in my gut, a red carpet.

"Where are we?" I ask Jonah.

I guess he can hear the panic in my voice, because he immediately offers me his arm and I take it, eagerly. To steady myself, if nothing else.

"It's a charity ball," he says. "Relax. You look amazing."

I manage to pick my way along the gauntlet of photographers and smiling reporters only because I have a vice-grip on Jonah's arm. I feel like I'm floating on a cloud of barely-concealed anxiety. Being on the red carpet has never, ever been a dream of mine. You know how some little kids dream about fame and celebrity? I was the opposite of that. I want to do math for a living and read great books while taking luxuriously lengthy baths.

"Jonah, who's the lovely lady?" someone yells.

I turn around to face a sea of cameras, flashes popping off everywhere. Jonah pulls me close with his hand around my waist.

"Smile," he tells me. "They just want a picture, then we can make a run for the door."

I plaster a smile onto my face and lean into Jonah on autopilot, startling at every flash. We're only there for a minute, but it feels like hours.

"You could have warned me," I hiss at Jonah as we finally begin to move again.

Jonah looks down at me and considers this for a moment.

"You're right," he concedes. "I didn't think about what a big deal it would be for you. Forgive me?"

"I guess it'll depend on how those photos turn out," I reply. "If I'm on the front page of some tabloid tomorrow looking like a deer in headlights, I may have to kill you."

"If it's any consolation, I was drunk in my first ever red-carpet pictures. Matt and I had just landed a big deal, our business was just taking off, and we decided to do some shots in the limo on the way. By the time we arrived we were totally smashed."

"Do you still have the photos?" I ask. "I might need some blackmail material in the near future. That way, at least I won't have to kill you. I can just keep you around for hot post-not-date not-sex."

He laughs. "I'm sure they're still out there, somewhere in the bowels of the internet."

"Fran!"

At the sound of the familiar voice, I spin around.

"Robbie!" I yelp. "Oh my God!"

I glance up at Jonah. He looks as pleased as punch, almost as delighted by my reaction as I am to see Robbie. She grabs me around my neck and pulls me into a tight hug.

"I didn't even know you were back from your vacation!" I exclaim, grinning.

"We got back last week," says Robbie. "And when Jonah found out we were going to be at the ball, he had no choice but to tell me you were coming too. I've been *dying* to text you all week, but I didn't want to spoil the surprise. You look *incredible*!"

"Thanks," I say, smiling sheepishly. I glance over my shoulder, but Jonah is already deep in conversation with Matt.

"So, you're dating, huh?" asks Robbie innocently, grinning from ear to ear. She is clearly very pleased with herself that her suspicions back on the island seem to have been proven correct.

"Uh," I say, looking back over at Jonah again. He's still not paying attention. "I… don't know," I admit, quietly. "I guess?"

Robbie laughs. "Well, 'uh, I don't know, I guess?' is a lot closer to dating than Jonah's ever gotten before. He must like you a lot." She hugs me again. "Which just proves that he's got impeccable taste!"

I smile back at her, so relieved that she's here with me amidst all this chaos. Jonah and Matt finally finish their conversation and come back over to join us.

"Shall we?" says Jonah, offering me his arm.

I look over at Robbie again. She gives me a reassuring nod, and I take a deep breath to steel myself.

"We shall," I say, and the four of us head inside.

❧

The ballroom is spectacular. Two huge crystal chandeliers are hanging from the ceiling, and opulent-looking drapery adorns every wall. The people all look amazing, and I even spot a few familiar celebrity faces milling around.

We're shown to our seats by a member of staff and immediately plied with bubbly, which we naturally accept. Robbie and I fall right into catch-up mode, me telling her all about awful Jessica and the report and her telling me all about her vacation and promising to forward Sarah's signed books as soon as she's home. She doesn't ask me about Jonah since he's *right there* beside me, occasionally running his finger down my bare back, and I don't tell her anything because I still feel pretty uncertain about what's going on with us myself.

The food, when it comes, is divine. There's a soup that's served by white-gloved waiters who pour it from little jugs into bowls lined sparsely with truffle shavings, the most delicate lemon and herb sea bass that I've ever tasted, and then a tiny lemon meringue pie to finish, which is decorated here and there with little flecks of gold. The portions are relatively small but satisfying. Robbie, who is by now a veteran of these events, tells me this is so that people won't feel too full to dance, mingle, and drink, so by the time the auction kicks off they'll be just the right combination of happy and blasted to really break out their wallets.

Some of the items being auctioned are incredible—there's a vacation to some far-off private island that was donated by a tech entrepreneur, a huge gift basket with the full range of a celebrity's new skincare line, and all manner of other wonderfully luxurious things. Even still, the amount of money that this crowd bids on them is enough to give someone like me vertigo. Robbie tells me that for some of the people here, it's a reputation thing; they don't want to be known as the cheapskate in the rich kids' club. But the proceeds are going to help with a food program for disadvantaged children, so whatever their motivation, it's still all going to a good cause.

Jonah and I haven't danced all night. I warned him in advance that I don't much enjoy dancing at public events like this one. I'm guessing he feels similarly because he immediately agreed that we wouldn't dance unless we both felt like it, and looked quite relieved. So we stay at the table most of the evening, talking, enjoying each others' company, and he keeps running his finger up my spine like it's a new tic he's just developed.

Some of the super-hot models I've seen in pictures with Jonah come over to say hi, and he introduces me to every one of them. A few of them stay a while to chat, and by the time they excuse themselves I feel a bit guilty for having thought badly of them before—and certain that Jonah was telling me the truth when he said they were just friends. One of them even complains to me that she had to come with "Edward Fucking Philmore" now that Jonah has a girlfriend. Jonah doesn't correct her about the girlfriend thing, and I'm too busy trying to remember where I know that name from. And then I remember that it's Goatee Guy from the party on the island, and I wince in sympathy with her.

"How about this?" asks Jonah, when the music turns slower and Ed Sheeran's *Thinking Out Loud* starts to play. "Shall we dance to this?"

I have a slight buzz from all the wine and merriment. The dance floor is full of couples, and Jonah has been the perfect gentleman all night.

"Sure," I say. "But I warn you, I have about four left feet."

"Excellent," says Jonah, getting to his feet and holding out his hand to me. "Me too. We can make a dancing spider and entertain everyone."

As soon as we're on the dance floor, Jonah pulls me close. There's something about being with him publicly, not in his apartment or on a desert island, not in a storm bunker or tucked away in the corner of a little-known restaurant, that makes it somehow more official.

But I try to remind myself that it's just one moment. Just one date. He lives in Chicago and I live in New York City, and I really have too much going on to make anything work with him. I almost killed myself this week trying to get one little report finished on time, and that's only going to get worse as I get more substantial projects to work on.

The music changes. *At Last* begins to play, and as Etta James' soulful voice floats over the dance floor, Jonah pulls me closer, pressing my body against his tightly, and we sway together. He runs his fingers up and down my spine and I lay my head against his chest, letting him lead me around the dance floor, weaving in and out between the throng of other couples.

When the night finally draws to a close, Jonah calls for Greg to pick us up while I hug Matt and Robbie goodbye.

"I'm so glad you were here," I whisper to her. "I don't know if I could've gotten through it otherwise."

She dismisses me with a wave of her hand. "You would've been fine," she whispers back. "And hopefully," she continues, looking meaningfully over towards Jonah, "We'll have more chances to see each other now."

I smile back at her, but my heart sinks a little. I'd love to see more of Robbie, but I just don't know if anything that long-term is in the cards for Jonah and me.

We get back to Jonah's apartment a little after 2am. Jonah is carrying my shoes because as soon as we were in the limo my feet finally rebelled and refused to wear those heels for a single second longer.

"Nightcap?" he asks.

"Sure," I say, flopping into a huge, comfy armchair. If I thought his apartment in Manhattan was nice, this place is something else. A penthouse—of course—huge and open plan, with fascinating pieces of art and sculpture dotted here and there in dimly lit alcoves. I make a mental note to examine them more closely when I'm not so dog tired.

It's been a long and busy few weeks. I sigh out a long breath and rest my head back on the chair.

And I don't wake up again until morning.

Chapter 16

"Oh my God," says Sarah, as soon as I step through the door of my office. "Where have you *been*?"

This seems like a weird question. I glance up at the clock to make sure I haven't accidentally missed the Daylight Savings Time changeover (again), but sure enough, it reads 9:03am. I turn back to Sarah and stare at her blankly.

"You mean, for the last three minutes?"

"Oh my God," she says again. She really over-uses that expression. "You haven't seen it?"

"Uh… I guess not?" I say. "What is 'it', exactly?"

Sarah picks up her phone and swipes it a few times, then turns it around to face me.

"It," it turns out, is me. In my beautiful designer dress, standing beside a billionaire on a red carpet, his arm draped around me.

"Hashtag Jonah's mystery girl is trending," says Sarah. "Look."

She swipes up and sure enough, there it is. #JonahsMysteryGirl. There are even a few articles speculating about who the unknown woman who finally bagged Jonah Wells could possibly be.

"Oh my God," I say. I can suddenly feel a rising panic behind my sternum.

"*Potts!*"

Jessica's voice comes booming from her office, even louder than usual. I physically cringe at the sound of it. Sarah is looking at me with the kind of expression that's usually reserved for a man who just got kicked in the nuts by a horse.

Feeling like all the blood has drained from my face, I turn and head slowly towards Jessica's office. I've heard some of the other employees refer to this section of the office, with its teal cubicle dividers and grass-colored recycling bins, as The Green Mile. I always thought it was just a stupid, unimaginative nickname, given the color scheme. But now... now, I understand.

"Yes?" I say as I enter, affecting as much innocent cluelessness as I can.

Jessica places one pristinely manicured hand on the laptop in front of her and turns it around. I'm looking at myself, once again—same dress, same red carpet... same billionaire.

"A friend of a friend," Jessica says, deadpan, echoing my words from a few weeks ago.

"I... uh."

"Of a friend," she adds, twisting the knife.

"Well, at the time," I say, carefully. "That was true."

"And now it's not," says Jessica, turning her laptop back around. It's a statement, not a question.

"Yes," I say, although Jonah and I didn't really make anything official. I don't know when our next meeting will be, or if it'll be a date, a not-date, or awkwardly running into each other at one of Matt and Robbie's parties. We just sort of left it at "we should do this again" when Greg picked me up.

"Right," says Jessica. "So, you need to get Wells to agree to run marketing for all his future acquisitions through us."

She says it so matter-of-factly, like she's just asking me to make a coffee. My mouth opens, but I'm too dumbfounded to say anything remotely coherent.

"Uh… I don't really…"

"And then we'll be able to make sure you get into the finance department here at the end of your first year," she says, staring straight at me, her voice perfectly even. "They don't always have enough places, you know?"

This awful, terrible, no-good *bitch*.

"Right," I say, lamely, my heart sinking.

"That's all," she says.

I turn to leave, feeling like I have a collection of rocks in the bottom of my stomach. I want nothing more than to get out of this room.

"Potts?"

"Yes?" I say, stopping in my tracks. I don't turn toward her. I might cry, and that wouldn't be professional. And I don't want to give her the satisfaction.

"Don't fail."

Boom. Another rock hits the pit of my stomach. I scurry out of the room without another word.

～

Jonah texts me on Thursday to ask if I want to stay in Chicago for the weekend. I don't tell him about Jessica and her wildly inappropriate demands. Or the new finance project she landed on my desk on Tuesday, which is about three times more work than the last one.

I tell him I'd love to go, but I'll have to bring some work with me. He says that's fine, and that Greg will pick me up from work at five on Friday.

When I turn up at work with my overnight bag on Friday, Jessica zeroes in on it immediately. She takes one look at the bag, looks me right in the eye, and tells me that she'll be expecting "an update on your little side-project" on Monday. I feel like I'm being pimped.

And there's no way in hell I'll be asking Jonah for work favors. I'll just have to figure out some way to handle Jessica without torching my chances at the accounting internship.

He's waiting in his apartment for me when I get there, like an island in a sea of chaos, and when I press myself against him, he wraps his arms around me tightly and squeezes.

"Hey," he says. "What's wrong?"

"Nothing," I say. "Work. Life. Stuff. I'm fine."

"You don't look fine, Franchesca," he says, holding me at arms' length. "I've made a dinner reservation, but I can cook if you'd rather st—"

"No," I say.

I resent Jessica's blackmail and I resent the fact that she's still piling work onto me and I resent the distance between Chicago and Manhattan, and I resent all the dumb articles that are still speculating about who I am. Not to mention the occasional calls I've started to get from random content creators looking for a scoop. But I'm sure as hell not going to let all that get in the way of a relaxing date-or-not-date —I don't care which—with the man I... like. A lot.

"Do I have time to get showered and changed?"

"Sure," he says. "Take your time. They'll hold the table for us anyway. Do you want me to pour you a drink while you're showering?"

"Yes," I say. "Thanks. That would be great. Just... anything that tastes like the weekend."

∿

I feel a little better by the time our entrees arrive in the small, intimate restaurant that Jonah's picked out. But it doesn't feel like real, deep relaxation, the kind I felt those first few days on the island. It's more like a veneer of calm over a roiling ocean of stress. Like peel-and-stick flooring, it's only a matter of time before the cracks start to show.

"I'll be in Manhattan in a few weeks," Jonah says. "You want to do dinner then?"

"Sure," I say without even thinking about it.

I guess we're dating now, if you can call it dating when we only get to see each other two or three times a month.

"Great. You want to pick the place?"

No. I don't want to pick the place. I'm absolutely up to my eyeballs trying to do two jobs at once and survive hell year and find a way to prevent Jessica from destroying my entire life plan, and I would rather pluck out my eyes with a fork than have to find the perfect little restaurant for us to go to.

"Sure," I say.

My phone starts to ring. I smile apologetically at Jonah and fish it out of my bag. My brows raise with surprise when I see who's calling.

"Hey, Brenda," I say as I lift the phone to my ear. "How are you?"

"Oh, hey Fran. I'm fine. Listen, dear, I don't want you to worry."

My stomach drops immediately. I've never heard Brenda start a call with those words.

"But your dad was taken into the hospital this afternoon."

"Oh, my God," I say as my stomach lurches again. "Why? Is he okay?"

Jonah is staring at me from across the table, concern etched across his face.

"It's his liver, dear," Brenda says. "He was looking very yellow when I went to give him his meds earlier, so I called the doctor and they ended up sending him into the hospital. They have him on an IV now. But the doctors say he should recover just fine as long as…"

She trails off and I feel my heart sink. I already know what she's going to say.

"As long as he stops drinking," I say, flatly.

"Yes, dear," says Brenda.

I close my eyes and swallow the lump that's formed in my throat. My dad has been slowly killing himself for years, and now it looks like he'll finally manage to pull it off.

"Alright, I'll be home as soon as I can."

"There's no need, Fran," she says. "There's nothing you can do."

"I know," I say. Nobody knows better than me that there's nothing I can do to help my dad. "But I want to."

Brenda is silent for a moment. "Okay dear, I understand. I'll make you up a bed. See you soon."

"Thanks, Brenda," I reply. "See you soon."

Jonah is leaning forward in his seat when I hang up, the concern carved even deeper into his features. "What's wrong?" he asks.

"My dad's in the hospital," I say, my voice shaking. "His liver is finally giving up."

What happens next is a bit of a blur. Jonah takes out his phone, and within thirty minutes we're both strapped into his plane on our way to Meadow Hill. I can see Lake Erie below, shimmering in the dusk. Jonah is a silent rock, wrapping his arm around my shoulders to steady me every time he sees me start to waver.

We arrive near midnight. Brenda and Anna are there to greet us, as are Robbie and Matt, who have come up from their mansion at the far end of town. The three women—my found family—all take turns wrapping me in tight hugs. Brenda makes tea, which is how she usually deals with stressful situations, and then she sits me down and quietly explains the prognosis. Visiting hours are long over, but we'll be able to go in and see my dad first thing in the morning.

"Do you want me to stay?" Jonah asks when we finally get a moment to ourselves.

"No," I say, shaking my head. "Thank you so much for bringing me here. I really appreciate it. But it'll be too cramped if you stay, and I'll mostly be at the hospital anyway."

"You're sure?" he says.

I nod. "Yeah. I'll let you know what happens. But you should head back."

He looks hesitant for a moment, but then he nods. "Alright. If you need anything at all I'm a few hours away at most. Do you want me to get Greg to come up here with the car so you can get around easier?"

"No," I say, though I'm touched by the offer. "Thank you. Brenda will drive me. And I'm sure Anna will let me borrow her car if I really need one. I'll be fine. But thank you for offering."

"Alright," says Jonah.

He, Robbie, and Matt take their leave a short while later, and I decide to try to get some sleep so I can get to the hospital early tomorrow.

A heavy wave of nostalgia washes over me as I open the door to Robbie's old room. But beneath that, there's a gut-churning sense of guilt. My mind is playing tricks on me, the way that minds often do when someone you have a complex relationship with is sick. I should have been here for my dad. I've been neglecting him, failing to call or text on time to tell him to take his meds, and not contacting

Brenda frequently enough to check in on him. I've failed him. And a tiny devil on my shoulder is telling me I did it on purpose. For payback. Because he failed me.

≈

I'm the first person to arrive at the hospital the next morning. Anna dropped me here because Brenda is working today. She also loaned me some of her clothes, which is why I'm wearing ripped jeans and a sweater that says "Let's get baked" under a picture of a gingerbread man. When she asks if I want her to come in, I shake my head.

"You go on. I'll stay for the day and get a bus back later."

"You sure?" she asks, hesitantly.

"Sure," I say, nodding.

She gives me a quick hug and I head inside, taking a deep breath before I go through the door. I hate hospitals. My most vivid memories of them all involve my mother, and all the treatments that made her sicker, and all the tubes and the beeps and the stench of disinfectant.

I'm so early that I have to wait for visiting hours to begin. When the doors finally open, I make my way down the corridor under the glare of the fluorescent strip lights, until I reach the nurse's station. A nurse accompanies me the rest of the way along the corridor and directs me into a side room.

There's my dad. A small and fragile man hooked up to tubes, surrounded by beeps. It's like a recurring nightmare.

"Hey," he says with a weak smile that doesn't reach his eyes.

He's sitting up in bed, and he's sober. And, Lord forgive me, I realize that I hate it when he's sober. When his mind is clear enough to actually feel bad about everything he's done and failed to do, and his face crumples up in permanent regret.

"Hey, Dad," I say, moving toward the bed. I bend down and hug him, quietly detesting the feel of his bony shoulder blades under my hands.

"No need for you to come, Fran," he says. "You should be in the city getting on with your life. You've earned all that."

"I'm not going to get on with my life while you're in the hospital, Dad," I say.

He looks away from me, out the window.

"They say you could recover completely if you stop drinking," I say, deciding to just get straight into it. I know how this scene plays out, and I don't have the mental energy to pussyfoot around it.

"Yeah," he says, nodding.

We fall into an awkward silence, letting the implication that he will not get better if he doesn't stop drinking hang in the air.

"So, tell me about the new job," he says when the silence has tortured us both enough.

It takes a while for the awkwardness to clear, but within an hour my dad and I are chatting just like we used to when I was younger. In his sobriety, he's able to pay attention to what I'm saying and respond enthusiastically. It's the most I've gotten out of him in years.

We head down to the cafeteria together, him dragging an IV stand beside him, and we talk more over sandwiches

216

and coffee. Soon, we're the only two left in the cafeteria, aside from a cleaner who's working around us, wiping down tables.

"I'm sorry, Franchesca," he says, out of nowhere.

I freeze. I'm not ready for the heavy stuff. I have too much going on. Too many strains already.

"Sorry for not being there. You needed me and I…"

"It's fine," I say quickly.

"It's not fine. Stop pretending you're fine. You've always done that."

"I'm surprised you noticed," I snap before I can stop myself.

My dad looks like I punched him in the gut, and I feel a heady mix of guilt and satisfaction. Whatever the feeling is, it's not healthy.

"I'm going to stop drinking," he says.

I've heard this before. I was even naïve enough to believe it the first few times.

"Sure, Dad," I say. "Probably a good idea."

He looks at me across the table, his eyes somehow younger than the abused shell he exists in. There's something like determination in his expression, but I'm not about to let myself go down that road again. Hope is a killer.

"Visiting hours are almost over," he says as I drain my coffee. "You get going now. And don't let me see you here tomorrow, you hear? You get back to your life."

I consider arguing with him, but I don't. I give him a peck on his cheek and walk him back to his room, and then I take my leave. I'll catch the bus back to Manhattan from town. I know Brenda would want me to go back to her place and stay another night, but I need some time alone to think and declutter my mind. And I'll get that on the bus.

Outside the hospital, the rain is coming down in sheets, and I don't have a coat or an umbrella with me. Just as I step out to hail a cab, an ambulance speeds by with its siren blaring, and its wheels plow right through a huge, muddy puddle at the side of the road. A torrent of silty water and mud explodes all over my shirt and pants.

"Jesus H. Christ!" I yell, jumping back.

I hear a distinctive click from somewhere nearby, and when I look around I see a squat, beady-eyed man standing there with a camera, leering at me.

"Hey!" I yell. I've just about had it with everything, and now this creep wants to get on my bad side.

I bolt toward him, my hand reaching out toward his camera, but he starts walking backward away from me with a click, click, click as he takes more pictures.

"Stop it!" I cry.

"Where's Jonah Wells?" he asks. "Want to give me an interview?"

"What?" I say, startling.

I realize with a jolt that this person, while he may be a creep, is not just some random creep who likes to take pictures of girls. He's a creep who's here *for me*, because of my relationship—if you can call it that— with Jonah.

"How did you know I'd be here?" I demand.

He doesn't answer. He snaps one more picture and then takes off at a jog down the sidewalk, pulling his hood up when he gets out from under the hospital's canopy.

"Fucking idiot," I say under my breath, and head back inside the hospital, where I use the facilities to make my best attempt at cleaning up and drying the wet mud.

When I head back outside, the sun is beaming and the skies are clear.

"Of course," I mutter under my breath and stick my arm out to hail a cab.

Chapter 17

By the time my alarm starts rattling my phone around my nightstand on Monday morning, I'm all thought out. I've thought endlessly all weekend, on the bus back to Manhattan, sitting around my apartment, in bed trying to get to sleep. Thinking about my dad, about Jonah, about the fact that I'm now apparently in the crosshairs of the paparazzi, about the internship, about what I'll do when I inevitably fail to meet Jessica's expectations regarding the seedy little "side project" she gave me. That one, at least, I'm perfectly happy to fail.

I'm probably not going to see Jonah for a while anyway, because I need to spend more time making sure my dad's okay. God only knows how long he'll be around if his liver is already failing. I spent a lot of yesterday googling for information about alcoholic hepatitis, and it's not good news. Especially for someone who keeps drinking.

Between my dad and work, all the traveling, and Jessica, whatever's going on between Jonah and me is starting to feel impossible.

I drag myself out of bed, and I manage to remember the little pile of signed books that Robbie sent me. I shove them into my bag and head for the subway.

"Hey," I call to Sarah as I walk into the office. Sarah is at her desk, staring up at me with her cheeks full. She swallows and pulls a bagel out from where she'd hidden it under the desk.

"Oh my God, don't do that!" she says. "I thought you were Jessica."

"I've got your books," I tell her, intent on putting the strain of the weekend behind me. I figure if I can make a positive start to the week, then I can focus on my work while I'm at work and leave everything else until later.

"Oh!" says Sarah, jumping to her feet with an eager grin. She takes the pile of books from me and flips to the first page of each, giving a little gasp each time she sees Robbie's name.

"Thank you sooo much for this!" she says to me, practically glowing. Then her smile fades a bit. "I'm not sure I should bring this up after you've just given me such a lovely gift, but... have you been online this morning? Checked your socials or anything?"

"No?" I say. "I try not to do that until after work." And even then, I prefer a good book to the insanity of social media.

"Ah," says Sarah, picking up her tablet and handing it to me with a grimace. As soon as I glance at the screen, my eyes go wide.

"*What the f—*"

"Busy, I hope?" asks Jessica, breezing in behind me en route to her office.

Sarah gives a little yelp and throws her bagel into the trash.

"Morning, Jessica!" she says, a little too eagerly.

I don't say anything, because I'm staring at a picture of myself in Anna's clothes, standing outside a hospital, covered in mud and rain, with my face contorted in anger. Except, the mud has so distorted the gingerbread man on the sweater that the "Let's get baked" pun is lost.

"SULLIVAN WELLS BILLIONAIRE'S DRUG-CRAZED HOOD RAT" screams the headline.

I can't even fathom why anyone would be interested in writing *anything* about me. But here it is, and all the career opportunities I saw in my future are swirling around a drain.

I know I shouldn't, but I scroll and read.

SCOOP! Turns out the girl who's been hanging on billionaire bachelor Jonah Wells' arm at every opportunity is a hood rat with an anger management problem!
When our photographer found Franchesca Potts outside a New York hospital—one that just *happens* to have a rehab program—she tried to attack him and steal his camera.

I've read enough. I put the tablet down and head for my desk, trying not to hyperventilate.

It'll be fine. I'm sure it'll be fine. It's just one dumb online mag. How bad could it be? And what sort of accountant would be found dead reading it? No one who's in a position to affect my future will know or care about this. It'll be fine.

The phone on my desk rings and I pick it up, glad for the distraction.

"Jessica Thorn's office," I say.

"Hey, can I speak to uh… Franchesca Potts?" asks a lilting man's voice on the other end of the phone.

"Speaking," I say.

"Hey, Jessica. My name's Alex. I work at Celeb E News. I was just wondering if you'd give us an interview about your rel—"

I slam the receiver back down, breathing hard, trying to gather my thoughts. There were enough of them bumping about in my head this morning already, but this bomb has just shattered them like shrapnel.

"You okay?" asks Sarah as she passes by with Jessica's morning coffee.

"I'm going to the bathroom," I say, grabbing my bag.

Inside the bathroom, I run into a cubicle and slam the door behind me, standing with my back against it and just *breathing*, trying to figure out exactly how bad this is and exactly what I can do about it.

I feel like my life has spiraled completely out of control. The last thing I can remember having any say in was what plant to buy for my moldy little apartment—and even that is sitting on the windowsill, wilted and brown because I've been neglecting it. Things can't go on like this. I have to do something. I have to do something that will make everything less complicated. If everything is less complicated, then I can get myself back on track. I could fix everything if everything was just simpler.

And just like that, a thought crystallizes in my mind. I hate it. I hate it because I know it will work. In a single stroke, it will wipe away almost every problem I have. But I hate it, and I fight against it for a long time before finally giving in.

I take my phone out of my bag and call Jonah.

"Hey!" he says when he answers. He sounds relaxed and happy to hear from me, which only makes me feel worse.

"Jonah, I can't do this," I blurt. "This long-distance dating thing. I can't. I've neglected my dad and work is falling apart, everything is spinning out of control and I just… I just can't. I think we should end it. I'll still see you at Matt and Robbie's parties. It's not you. It's me. We'll be friends."

My heart is thundering and tearing in two at the same time. I stop speaking, and nothing happens. The other end of the line is dead silent. It's so silent for so long that I begin to think I've been disconnected.

"Hello?" I say.

"Okay," says Jonah.

Just that. *Okay.* I don't know what I was expecting—for him to argue with me? But now that I've said it and he has so easily accepted it, I can hardly take it back. Maybe it's for the best. My head tells me it is. My heart is strangling me so hard that I can't speak.

"Okay," I croak.

"Anything else?" Jonah asks, his voice shifting immediately into a detached, professional-polite tone.

"No," I say.

"Okay," he says.

I can't say anything else, and I can feel a huge swell surging up behind my sternum. I can't let Jonah hear it come out, so I hit the button to end the call and slap my hand over my mouth to muffle the sob that erupts from me.

I sit in the bathroom stall for a long time, trying to make the tears stop. But I can't. And even if I could, I can't make my face look less blotchy or my makeup less ruined.

I go back to my desk, keeping my head down.

"Tell Jessica I'm sick," I say to Sarah, barely holding myself together.

"Are you alright?"

"I'll be fine," I lie, and head for the door.

I get a lot of weird looks on the train. I guess I *do* look weird. It's not every day you see a woman in a designer suit, crying alone on the subway.

By the time I reach my apartment, I already know I've done something really stupid. The panic of that moment —of seeing myself in that tabloid rag with that headline, of getting tracked down *at work* by some shitty celebrity gossip show—has subsided enough for me to realize that I acted out of desperation, not because of some epiphany. Sure, I made things simpler—but there is any number of other things I could have tried instead. I didn't have to throw the billionaire out with the bathwater.

But he didn't have to say "okay". What sort of response is that? Maybe it's for the best after all, if it was that easy for him to come to terms with it. Maybe I need this. I'll have more time for work. More time for visits home. No more paparazzi buzzing around. And an ironclad excuse for why I can't use my boyfriend to get Sullivan Wells' business.

More of a lot of things.

But a lot less Jonah.

I flop down onto my bed and cry my heart out.

Chapter 18

"Hello?" I say out loud, just to make sure my voice still works.

It's Wednesday, and I haven't spoken to anyone since I rushed home on Monday morning. I sent Sarah a message on Tuesday to tell her I had a terrible stomach bug and didn't know if I'd be in for the rest of the week. She replied very professionally and then sent me a separate text message to see if I was okay, which I didn't reply to.

Brenda called yesterday as well, but I couldn't bear to answer. So I ignored it, and then she sent me a message to let me know my dad was home.

I've been in the same pajamas for three days, trying to sort my head out. I've told myself that ending things with Jonah is for the best. We live in separate cities and lead massively different lives. I don't believe myself, but I keep repeating it regardless.

My phone rings just after dinner time. It's Robbie. I take a deep breath and pick it up.

"Hey," I say.

"Hey," she says. "Are you home from work? I didn't want to bother you while you were busy."

"I'm not," I say. "Is everything okay?"

"Oh, yeah. I was just calling to check if the books got to you."

"Yep," I say. "They got here fine."

"What's wrong?"

She knows me far too well.

"Nothing," I say. "I'm fine. I'll be home this weekend."

I've been hemming and hawing about it, but I really do need to check on my dad and start spending more time with him. If I don't at least do that, then what was the point of shredding my heart and breaking things off with Jonah?

"Oh, great!" says Robbie. "Is Jonah coming with you?"

My heart leaps at the mention of his name and then flops back down like a dead fish. He hasn't told Robbie. Which means he hasn't told Matt. So I guess he really is as nonplussed as he sounded on the phone.

Even though it was me that ended it, I really wish he was more bothered. Which is unreasonable, I know, but I never claimed to be a Stoic.

"Hello?" says Robbie.

"Uh, no," I say. "I don't think I'll be seeing him again. Apart from your stuff, you know. Parties and things."

"Oh, no!" says Robbie, sounding way more concerned than Jonah did. "What happened?"

"Nothing. I just…" I trail off because I can feel a painful throb in my throat, and I know that if I tell Robbie what an absolute idiot I've been, I'll cry. "Tell you on the weekend?"

"Sure," she says. "But you're okay?"

"I'll be okay," I say. "I'm just busy with work."

"Awful Jessica on your case?" she asks.

"Yeah," I say, trying and failing to lift my voice. "Something like that."

"Okay. Matt's in Manhattan on Friday. You want to hitch a ride on the helicopter?"

I try to imagine spending time making small talk with Matt. Again, I know it's unreasonable, but I can't help feeling a little bitter towards him for his role in all this. If he hadn't been pestering Jonah to date me, then nothing would have happened between us. And if nothing had happened between us, Jonah would still be the untouchable billionaire I occasionally fantasize about, instead of the man who made me feel like the world was made of better things, and then didn't so much as flinch when I dumped him in a moment of crisis.

I still cringe every time I think about it.

"No," I say. "I'll make my own way. But thanks."

"Alright," says Robbie. "See you on the weekend, then. Dinner at mine on Saturday?"

"Sure," I say, hoping I'll have gotten over this emotional fragility by then. "Sounds great."

"Okay. Love you."

"Love you, too," I say, and hang up.

I get to my dad's house on Friday evening, having traveled through the day. I still haven't returned to work; I'm just not ready for it yet. I'd probably cry if Jessica started giving me the third degree about Sullivan Wells or any of my ongoing projects.

My dad opens the door looking remarkably healthy. And sober.

"Hey," I say, the surprise evident on my face.

He looks completely delighted to see me.

"Franny!" he grins. "Come in, come in."

The house I grew up in looks so different from the last time I was here. There are no empty beer cans or bottles strewn around, no crumb-covered plates. The lamps all have bulbs in, casting a warm glow around the room, and the cushions on the sofa look clean and newly fluffed.

"Wow," I say, looking over at my dad, who is watching me nervously. "Did you do all this? Aren't you supposed to be resting?"

"Brenda helped me," he says. "She came by and gave me an earful about worrying you. And made me finally hear some truths I should have listened to a long time ago."

"You're sober?" I ask.

"No," he says.

I raise a brow.

"I'm an alcoholic, Franchesca."

My legs almost give way beneath me. He's occasionally said things like "I have a bit of a problem" or "I could drink a bit less" or "I'm going to stick to light beers," but this... this is completely new.

His hair is combed, I notice. And his trousers are pressed.

"And I always will be," he continues. "But I haven't had a drink since the day they brought me into the hospital. Brenda took me down to the AA yesterday and I got a sponsor. You know Willy from the hardware store?"

"Dad," I say, "Are you for real?"

He pauses and frowns, looking down at his feet.

"Fran, I don't deserve a second chance. Lord knows I don't, after how I failed you when your mom passed. But I got one. So, I'm going to make the most of it. And I'm going to earn your trust back."

I'm suddenly overwhelmed with emotion. This is so different from all the times that came before. It's not that I'm certain he'll pull it off—I know the stats on alcoholics and relapses—but his sincerity in wanting to try, instead of being cajoled and nagged and browbeaten into a half-hearted stay in rehab... I let myself hope a little.

I can feel hot tears pricking my eyes. A big, fat droplet rolls down my cheek and drops right off my chin onto my sweater.

"Hey," says my dad, coming closer. He pulls me into the sort of hug he used to give me before my mom died and the light went out of his eyes, and I bawl my eyes out on his shoulder. The stress of work, the sadness over Jonah, the years and years of pent-up pain from missing my dad... it all comes pouring out of me in a torrent.

"It'll be okay," he soothes, stroking my hair. "It'll all be okay."

He guides me to the sofa and holds my hand until I pull myself together. He asks me to tell him everything about my life in the city, and I spend hours making him hate a woman called Jessica who he's never met.

~

The night I spent talking with my dad, realizing that he actually does seem committed to change this time, has done me no end of good (though the opportunity to bitch unreservedly about Jessica may also have helped). We're not at the point where we can talk about the past yet—even all these years later, talking about mom is too raw a subject for him—but I'm hopeful that, in time, we can get there.

I get ready for dinner at Robbie's house and resolve not to talk about Jonah unless it's brought up. And I try to remind myself that Matt is not a bad guy so that I don't try to throttle him in the very likely event that it *is* brought up. I tell my dad that I'll stay at Robbie's house for the night and head back to the city from there on Monday because I don't want to come back to his house smelling of wine. He hugs me goodbye, and we part on good terms for the first time in forever.

Robbie's house still blows me away. I came here a few times when I was young, when it was still owned by a man named Lincoln O'Neill, but it looks nothing like it did back then. It's all modern décor, and it has Robbie's stamp all over it. There's an occasional accent cushion or a chair with some amazingly bold pattern on it, but otherwise, she's given the rooms depth with textures; wood, wicker, linen, cotton, and brushed metals. The dining room is just the right size to accommodate the large, round table in the middle, but small enough to feel intimate and cozy.

The chef has prepared a lovely charcuterie board for us, with home-baked bread and lots of different dipping oils. It's perfect for a casual evening in, and Robbie, Matt, and I all dig in as we chat our way through dinner.

"Your dad sure does seem determined to make a change," says Matt, after I tell them about how he's doing.

"Yeah," I say. "It's still early days, but visiting him yesterday was like night and day compared to the last time I was home."

"So, what happened with Jonah?" asks Robbie, who can be every bit as blunt as her sister Anna when she wants to be.

The question I've been dreading all night hangs in the air for a moment. I glance at Matt, who is staring studiously at his wine glass, then back to Robbie.

"Nothing, really," I say, focusing every ounce of energy I have on keeping my voice level and my tone casual. Just like Jonah did. "It was just… different places, different lifestyles. You know how it goes."

Both of them, despite having started off in different places with wildly different lifestyles themselves, nod. I'm slightly relieved that I've managed to escape this question with only a vague platitude.

"He told me he doesn't date, anyway," I say. "He only really started a thing with me because Matt was nagging him to."

There goes my mouth. Too late to reel it back in now.

"What?" says Robbie, looking from me to Matt.

"It wasn't like that," says Matt, looking slightly uncomfortable at the revelation that I know he was pestering Jonah. "And he doesn't date. Not since Gianna."

"Who's Gianna?" asks Robbie, much to my relief. I would never have asked, but I would never have stopped wanting to know.

Matt sighs and puts his wine glass down.

"It's not really my place t—"

"Who's Gianna?" repeats Robbie. I can't quite put my finger on it, but something about her tone clearly conveys that she's invoking her wife card on Matt.

Matt hesitates, then sighs again. "Gianna was the girl he was engaged to in college," he says.

I nearly choke on my own wine. The Jonah I know is not a man who would ever have been engaged. I lean forward a little and listen with rapt attention as Matt continues.

"She was beautiful, outgoing, smart, charismatic… really, it was little wonder that he fell for her. But as time went on, it became clear that she was also highly manipulative and terribly, almost sociopathically self-centered. After months of stringing him along, she finally got together with him just as it became obvious our business was going to take off. At the time, it just seemed like everything was starting to go right for him, and he was ecstatic. Of course, it wasn't a coincidence. She nearly drained him of every penny he earned in our first year. But he was into her. I guess… I don't know. He has a big heart."

Matt sighs again. But this time, it's sadder, almost like he's mourning his friend.

"Or at least, he did before Gianna. Anyway, he was blind to what was going on, and whenever I or anyone else raised any concerns he just brushed them off. About a year and a half in, he got engaged to her. And then, two months before the wedding, his mom died in a car accident. Just, there one minute and gone the next. He was devastated. Inconsolable. But Gianna was not about to let a little thing like her fiancé's grief derail her big day. So when Jonah asked—pleaded with her, really—to postpone the wedding, she broke up with him. By text message."

"Oh my God," says Robbie.

I don't say anything.

"She gave him all the usual lines. You know, 'it's not you, it's me', and 'we can still be friends', and so on. And then, barely a week later, she announced her engagement to some Wall Street high-flyer."

Matt drains his whiskey. There's a grim expression on his face.

"They ended up getting married in the venue she'd picked out for her and Jonah. On the same day."

Robbie doesn't say anything. She just leans back in her chair and exhales.

I don't say anything, either. I can't. I'm frantically running over my breakup with Jonah in my head. *It's not you. It's me. We'll still be friends.*

I can't breathe.

"As you can imagine, that broke him. He was humiliated, of course, but the main thing was that he just couldn't understand how a person who to him seemed so charming could turn out to be so… *mercenary*. And so I think he just decided it was safer not to try. He started taking model friends to parties to keep other women away, and he never seemed interested in anyone. Until he met you," he says, looking over at me.

I swallow. Hard. There's a huge lump in my throat and it won't budge.

"I'm sorry if I caused you any trouble, Fran," says Matt. "It wasn't my intention. But when he told me that if he were ever to date anyone again, it'd be you... well, it was like watching a part of my friend come back to life." He sighs again. "Anyway, I shouldn't have interfered. I apologize."

"I need some air," I croak, rising from my seat.

As I'm walking toward the back door I can hear Robbie whispering something to Matt, but I can't make out what it is. She doesn't sound pleased.

I press my back against the wall outside and look up at the sky.

If I had known, would I have acted differently? Maybe. But I would at least have understood Jonah's terse response, and his instant switch to cool professional detachment. Christ, it must have been such an awful flashback for him. At the very least, maybe I could have softened the blow.

Would've, could've, should've. All my thought experiments are pointless now, anyway. Jonah won't be interested in trying again after I've dredged up this horrible crap from his past, and I'm not sure I blame him.

I miss him. But I don't blame him.

I let out a sigh and feel something like acceptance flow through me. Or maybe this is the feeling I've been running from since I was a little girl: helplessness. Defeat.

"You okay?"

Robbie puts her hand on my shoulder and squeezes it.

"I will be," I say.

I'll double-down in work, I decide. I will kick hell year's ass and get my damn position in the accounting department next year, and I'll make Jessica watch me do it. I'll focus on supporting my dad, and I'll come back to Meadow Hill more often to water the roots I've been trying so hard to run away from.

"Yeah," says Robbie, pulling me into a hug. "You always are."

Chapter 19

I've been back at work for just over a month, and everything is going... okay, I guess. Jessica gave me some grief about not being able to get any further with Sullivan Wells, but she seemed to grudgingly accept that "we broke up" was a pretty watertight excuse, and I think ordering me to get back with Jonah would've been a step too far even for her. Instead, she gave me two additional projects to work on and "volunteered" me to help her organize a fundraising event for one of AJX's charity partners. It's a lot, but I've been managing to catch up on work in the evenings and on weekends now that I don't have to travel to see Jonah anymore.

I don't think about him that often anymore. Maybe once every couple of hours. I still miss him, but the wound has scarred over to the point where it's now more of a dull ache than a sharp pain.

My dad is doing well. He emailed me a picture of his red chip a few days ago—thirty days sober. If you'd asked me a year ago, I never would have believed it. He's taken up photography and gardening again, so he's sent me a few nice pictures of a little vegetable patch he's started growing in his backyard.

"Potts!"

"Jesus," I hiss, looking up at Jessica, who has pulled her classic apparate-right-beside-my-desk trick.

"I have an emergency," she says.

She actually does look slightly flustered. There's a single hair out of place on the left side of her head.

"Okay," I say.

"One of the models has dropped out for tonight. Appendicitis or something."

"The auction models?"

She's talking about the charity event we've been organizing. In a very on-brand move, Jessica decided that she wanted to auction *people* at her fundraiser.

She doesn't answer my question. Obviously.

"You'll have to do it," she says.

"What?" I ask, blinking at her.

"The auction. You'll have to be auctioned. Don't worry, they hardly ever actually go on the date."

"No!" I blurt, standing up. "I can't do that! It's... I'm not a model, I'm an intern!"

"You can and you will," says Jessica, narrowing her eyes. She really is stressed. She almost has a worry line breaking through the botox on her forehead. "You can wear that dress you wore on the red carpet with Jonah Wells."

I feel a vein start to pulse in my forehead, and I briefly wonder if I look as stressed as Jessica does. Why does this man's name keep coming back to haunt me?

"Jessica," I say, trying to sound stern. Our relationship has become a touch more frank over the last month. "I can't do this."

"Potts," she says. "If you do it, I will make sure you're in finance next year."

"You're an evil woman," I tell her, plainly.

"And you're a brilliant accountant," she says, turning to stride back to her office. "Don't waste it."

Perhaps you'll understand how panicked I am when I tell you that I don't even register the fact that Jessica—*Jessica!* —just paid me a compliment. I grab my phone and rush to the bathroom.

"Robbie!" I practically shout when she picks up.

"Hey Fran, I'm jus—"

"You have to help me," I say, interrupting her. "One of the models dropped out of this fundraiser I'm helping with and *fucking Jessica* is making me be in the auction. I am going to *be* auctioned."

"Fran, I—"

"I can't be in the auction. I'm not a model! She told me to wear that dress I wore to the charity ball."

"Well, you did look amazing," says Robbie.

"I don't need compliments, I need help!" I hiss. "Why did I take this job, Robbie? Why? God. What am I going to do?"

"You'll be fine," she says. "Breathe."

"She said if I do it, she'll make sure I get a place in Finance next year."

"Wow," says Robbie.

"Right?!" I say. "She's so ruthless I almost admire her. God. This sucks. I'm going to have to walk my frumpy ass over that stage with a bunch of supermodels. Their asses are amazing, that's their whole job! And I have knock knees, Robbie. Knock knees! And that dress just reminds me of—"

"*Fran,*" she says sternly, cutting me off.

"Yeah, yeah," I say, squeezing the bridge of my nose. "Breathe. I know." I exhale deeply and try to calm down. "What are you doing, anyway?"

"As I've been trying to tell you," she says, carefully. "I'm having lunch with Matt and Jonah."

I fall silent, thinking back over the conversation. And then my stomach fills with dread.

"Am I on speakerphone?"

"No."

I let out a gasp of relief. "Oh, thank God."

"But you're shouting so loud that everyone can hear you anyway."

"Fuck!" I say, and hang up.

∾

I show up at the venue—the ballroom of a local hotel, which is gorgeous and suitably posh, but not nearly on the same level as my last charity event—around nine. The auction is right at the end of the night, by which point everyone will have been suitably lubricated, and I have no desire to show up any earlier than necessary and risk having to mingle or make small talk. I really just want to get there, get this humiliating ordeal over with, and get off the stage as quickly as possible. I hand my garment bag to Sarah, who is in charge of wardrobe for all the auction models, and head into the makeshift green room behind the stage.

Robbie has sent me a few texts apologizing for earlier, and I've replied to say it's fine. I didn't call, because then she'd be able to tell that I'm still annoyed. But I'm annoyed because I know I still care about what Jonah thinks of me, and I don't want to admit that. Even to myself.

I spend the next hour or so sitting quietly in the green room, reading, sipping water, and avoiding Jessica's gaze any time she's in the vicinity. The last thing I need is for her to get any more bright ideas about how I can "help" in exchange for a position on the Finance team.

A little after ten, Sarah announces that the auction will be starting in an hour. She rolls out a long clothes rack with all our garment bags hanging from it, arranged in order of appearance.

"I've put you last," she says to me, quietly. "So fewer people will still be paying attention." She gives me a sympathetic look. "You'll be fine, Fran. Just think of next year."

Think of next year. Think of next year. I start repeating it in my head like a mantra.

The next hour is a flurry of activity as everyone in the tiny green room starts getting ready. There's a lot of makeup to be applied and a limited number of mirrors available. A few people are doing what I assume is Pilates to limber up; others are practicing their catwalk strut. The models are actually very nice, at least the ones I talk to, but I still feel horribly out of place.

The auction kicks off at eleven. I head to the side of the stage to watch the first one just so I know what to expect. The woman who steps onto the stage is a willowy wonder, all limbs and eyelashes, and she looks amazing in a floor-length white gown that's split practically to her waist. I recognize her from some cosmetic advertising campaign that AJX ran a while back.

"Our first lot," says Jessica, looking ever the professional host. "Is Yeva Zubko, a professional model from the West Village who's also an avid sailor and a former champi-onship volleyball player!"

Of course she is. Good for her.

Yeva gives a little wave and stands on the stage with her hand on her hip like a pageant queen, looking out toward the audience, radiating confidence. This is nothing to her.

"We'll start the bidding at one thousand dollars," says Jessica.

I look out into the sea of people and spot a little white sign going up.

"I have a thousand dollars," says Jessica. "Do I hear fifteen hundred?"

Another sign goes up right away. The bids keep coming thick and fast until a date with Yeva is sold for nineteen thousand dollars. I'm blown away by the amount. I figure I'll be lucky if someone pays ten for me. Dollars, not thousands.

The second lot is a male model named Frederico, who is sold to a very eager, grey-haired lady in a glittering red dress for twelve thousand.

With a slight lurch of my stomach, I decide it's time to head backstage and get dressed because there are only seven more lots before I'm up.

I pick up my garment bag from the green room and head to the changing area. But when I pull down the zipper and see dusky pink fabric instead of the burnt orange of my red-carpet dress, I feel an immediate surge of panic.

"Sarah," I say looking around. "Sarah?" I call again, louder this time.

But Sarah is nowhere to be seen, and all the other auction models are lined up ready to take their turn on the stage. I quickly scan over them. None are wearing burnt orange, so it can't be that my dress just got mixed up with one of theirs.

"Shit," I hiss. This is the last thing I need right now.

I pull the garment bag open wider to get a better look at the dress. As I do, a dim feeling begins to form somewhere at the back of my mind, as though I've... seen this dress before? I wonder if it's like when I recognized Yeva. Is this dress from one of our marketing campaigns? No, that doesn't seem right.

I'm still hesitant to just pull it out of the bag since I don't know who it belongs to. My eyes trail over the dress, straining to figure out where I've seen it before, until they eventually settle on a small, intricately-detailed embroidered flower. The dim feeling deep in the recesses of my mind suddenly explodes in recognition, even as my conscious mind fights back against the idea, for the simple reason that it's impossible.

Me. The dress belongs to me. It's my dress. The one I wore when I was maid of honor at Robbie's wedding.

My mouth falls open. How is that even possible? Not hesitating anymore, I pull the dress all the way out of the bag to look at the whole thing.

There's no doubt about it; it's the same dress. But it looks way better than the last time I saw it. The little embroidered parts that had been stained with pond weed are completely clean, almost like the embroidery has been redone from scratch. And all the light stains on the skirt are gone. The entire dress is pristine. Better than new.

My brain still isn't ready to accept this. Maybe it *is* a different dress? It was supposed to be one-of-a-kind, but maybe the deal was that the designer could make more of them after the wedding? I suddenly realize there's a way to find out for sure. I reach into the dress and fish around inside it… and sure enough, there's a tiny, silk tag inside that has "F.P." embroidered into it. It's *the* dress.

"What the *actual fu*—"

"And now for lot nine!" I hear Jessica call.

"Oh my God, you're not dressed!" Sarah yelps, appearing right beside me. "Quick, you're up next!"

I blink at her, and it takes me a moment to remember where I am and what I'm supposed to be doing. I leap into action, tearing off my sweater and jeans and shimmying into the gown.

It fits me perfectly. Well, why wouldn't it? It's *my* dress.

My phone rings right when I'm halfway into my dress. I reach out and hit the speaker button.

"Hey, Robbie," I say, slightly out of breath. "What's up?"

"I just wanted to call to say sorry about earlier again," says Robbie. "I felt so bad. Are you alright?"

"I'm fine," I say, half-grunting as I yank the gown up. "Did I say anything mortifying? I've been trying to replay the conversation in my head."

"Don't forget to wave when she tells everyone about you," whispers Sarah as she zips me up.

"No," says Robbie. "Jonah took off right after you called. Didn't even finish his lunch. Have you been auctioned yet?"

I don't really want to talk about Jonah, beyond confirming that I didn't make a *complete* idiot of myself earlier. Luckily, I have the perfect excuse to change the subject.

"No, I'm just getting dressed. Oh, hey!" I say. "You'll never guess what."

"What?"

Sarah takes my arm and pulls me over to the side of the stage.

"You know the dress from your wedding? The one I sold?"

"Yeah?"

"Well, I'm wearing it. Right now. It was in my garment bag."

"Wait, *what?*" says Robbie, sounding absolutely dumbfounded. I'm glad I'm not alone.

"I know!" I say. "I have no idea what's going on."

I turn to Sarah.

"Sarah where did this dress come fr—"

I don't get to finish the question, because Sarah chooses that moment to push me out into the glare of several spotlights so bright that I recoil like a vampire and quickly raise my hand to shield my eyes. Even then, I still can't see anyone in the audience. I have to squint to even make out the rest of the stage.

Realizing that my phone is still in the hand that I just raised to blot out the spotlights, I quickly hit the button to end the call and shove the phone down the front of my dress. With a deep breath, I straighten myself up to try and salvage this thing before it goes any further off the rails.

Jessica does not look at all impressed by my entrance. She clears her throat and begins to introduce me.

"Franchesca Potts is a promising accounting intern at AJX who graduated top of her class in high school and college. She enjoys reading and… wine," says Jessica, with a note of disapproval and a withering glance at me.

She asked me to write down my hobbies. She didn't say they had to be interesting.

A ripple of chuckling passes through the crowd, and I shift self-consciously on my feet. I have no idea what sort of pose I'm pulling, but I do know that I look nowhere near as elegant as Yeva did. And the fact that I'm still mystified by exactly how this gown came to be in my garment bag isn't helping my focus.

"Shall we start the bidding at a thousand dollars?" asks Jessica.

I can't see the audience, so I'm completely reliant on Jessica's vocal cues to know how it's going.

"I'm bid one thousand dollars. Fifteen hundred?"

There's a hush around the room. Oh, God. There's a *hush*.

And then, just when the silence has lasted long enough to make it *especially* embarrassing, my phone starts ringing.

"Shit," I hiss, giving Jessica a groveling look as I pull the phone out of the front of my gown—like a real classy lady at a fancy charity auction—and answer it. I can't do anything else. Robbie will just keep trying if I don't.

I hold the phone to my ear. "Hey, Robbie."

"The call cut off," says Robbie, and I immediately tear the phone away from my ear as her voice comes through about ten times louder than I was expecting. Because of course, it's still on speakerphone from the last call.

There's another ripple of chuckling from the crowd, but it's *significantly* closer to laughter this time. I turn my back to them to talk to Robbie.

"I, uh… I can't really talk right now."

"Ohhh, are you about to be auctioned?"

"I'm… currently being auctioned," I say, cringing.

"Oh, shit," says Robbie, and the crowd breaks into a torrent of outright laughter.

I glance over at Jessica. She looks like a ball of condensed rage. Her forehead vein is popping out so much that it looks like she's sprouting a twin.

"Yeah, gotta go," I say.

"Knock 'em de—"

With Robbie cut off, I turn back around and shove my phone back down the front of my dress.

"Sorry about that," I say, with a weak, grimacing smile.

"Fifteen hundred dollars?" says Jessica into her microphone, through gritted teeth.

Nothing. Silence. I can feel a cringe beginning to wriggle out along my limbs as if urging me to curl up into a ball. I knew this was a horrendous mistake. I should have pretended to have salmonella or something.

"One million dollars."

Time seems to stop, suddenly. I still can't see anything, and my mind is still burning with too much humiliation to really process what it just heard, but the cringe that had its tendrils around my limbs starts to turn into a tingle, as if my body already knows something I don't. I hear Sarah gasp from the other side of the curtains behind me.

"Uh… what?" says Jessica.

I look over at her, and she has a hand up to shield her eyes from the spotlights. She's squinting out at the audience, which is suddenly alive with little gasps and murmurs.

"One million dollars," repeats the voice, closer this time, and it's all the confirmation I need. I'd recognize that voice anywhere.

I see his leg first, stepping up onto the stage as if emerging from a halo of light. I am frozen to the spot, my heart hammering in my chest. I haven't seen him in what feels like forever, but he hasn't changed a bit. He's still the same big, beautiful man, his blue eyes sparkling fantastically in the spotlights. I feel an involuntary smile blooming on my face as tears spring to my eyes.

"Can I just confirm that you're bidding one million dollars?" says Jessica into the microphone.

"I'm so sorry," I blurt, the tears suddenly breaking free and falling down my cheeks. I don't care how many people are watching. I must tell him. I must let him know that I'm sorry for what I did, and what I said.

But my apology seems to take him by surprise. His brows draw down as he takes a step closer.

"What do you mean, sorry?" he asks. "It's me who should be sorry."

"No!" I say, a little too loud, maybe. "It's me. I'm sorry for... for..."

I don't want to say anything that's not mine to say in front of a room full of people who are probably business contacts for Jonah. You could hear a pin drop in here right now.

"Franchesca," says Jonah, carefully, and just the sound of my name on his lips draws a sob from me. "You're sort of screwing up my big groveling apology here."

"*Your* apology?" I say. The tears are still streaming down my face and I'm laughing. I must look like a real lunatic.

"Hi there." I have to stifle a yelp as Jessica suddenly appears right beside us. "Sorry to interrupt... whatever this is, but could I just get you to confirm that you are, in fact, bidding one million dollars?"

"Yes," says Jonah sharply, turning to look right at Jessica. I've never actually seen her speechless before. I like it.

"Can we go and talk?" asks Jonah, turning back to me.

I'm feeling every kind of emotion at once, and I'm not sure how to handle it. It's overwhelming. So I nod dumbly and turn to head back through the curtains with him.

"Let's have some more music!" I hear Jessica call, as we walk past a very intrigued-looking Sarah to the green room.

Chapter 20

"I'm so sorry," I blabber as soon as the door closes behind Jonah. My heart is racing and every thought in my mind is pouring out of my mouth.

"The way I... the way I broke up with you... I was just so stressed out and I felt like everything was happening at once and I was completely irrational and... and... I know you can't forgive me. But I need you to know I never would have done it like that or said those things if I... Matt told me about Gianna. I just didn't know how t—"

I stop talking abruptly because Jonah presses his finger against my lips.

"Stop," he says quietly.

I stop, looking up at him through a haze of tears, battling to hold back the words that are clawing at my tongue.

"Franchesca, listen to me. Gianna is nothing to me now. For a long, long time, she cast such a looming shadow over my life, and I got so used to living in the dark. And then I met you, and you exploded into my life like a firework, and

I… it just took me a long time to get used to the light again."

He takes a deep breath, his eyes to the ceiling, and sighs it out.

"I should have said something sooner. Before you had to overhear Matt trying to convince me to man up and tell you how I felt."

"That did sort of suck," I say with a sniffle.

"Yeah," he nods, with a whisper of a smile. "Or the day of the treasure hunt, when you told me about your mom, and all I wanted to do was hold you so tight that you'd never have to carry that pain alone again."

I stare up at him, trying to make sense of what he's saying.

"Or the night you brought me a blanket and I pretended to be sleeping because I was too chickenshit to tell you how I felt."

I've stopped crying now. I'm listening intently, hooked on every word he's saying.

"You were awake?" I croak.

"Or the day you arrived on the island when I saw you right in front of me on that beach, and it was like I could finally breathe again after a year of suffocating. Or when I arranged the Hong Kong meeting so you'd get an extra day on the island, because you deserve paradise, Franchesca. More than anyone."

I'm trying to think back to the island, to all the times we almost kissed, all the times he pulled away. "Jonah, I—"

He shakes his head and presses his finger to my lips again.

"I should have told you when I bought your dress from Castoff Couture."

I gasp and look down at my dress. I only mentioned Castoff Couture to him once, months before I listed the dress for sale. And he remembered. And he bought it.

And I guess he somehow managed to switch it with the dress I brought with me tonight.

Something is changing inside me with each new revelation, and it's the most bizarre sensation I've ever felt. Every interaction I've ever had with Jonah is being recast in a new light. Every smile, every glance, every word we've ever shared in the past feels different now. More… significant, somehow.

"I should have dragged you into my bed down in Florida after you fell in the lake."

I grin at him, my eyes brimming with tears. "You wouldn't have had to drag me."

He smiles. "But most of all, I should have told you that I'd fallen completely, hopelessly in love with you in an instant, the very first moment I saw you in Robbie's house, when you had your hair in a big mess on top of your pretty head, and you were wearing pajamas and a tank top and a gorgeous smile."

"I told Robbie I'd slide down you like a fire station pole," I blurt.

Jonah lets out a full belly laugh. "I was the biggest idiot of all to let you go the way I did. I knew you were hurting, stressed out, and anxious. I shouldn't have left you in Meadow Hill when your dad was sick. And when you called me and told me you didn't think we could work, I shouldn't have made out like I didn't care. Because I do care, Franchesca. I care a lot."

"I can be pretty irrational," I say, sniffing.

"You can be *wildly* irrational," says Jonah, smirking.

I raise a brow at him.

"Seriously," he says. "Mad as a box of frogs."

I laugh at that, and the laugh is as cathartic as the tears were just a moment ago. But as relief floods over me, I jolt back to reality with a start.

"Oh my God!" I say. "You just bid a million dollars! You'd better go and tell Jessica you weren't serious."

"I was deadly serious," he says. "You picked the charity, right? Breast cancer research?"

"Yes," I say.

"For your mom," he says, quietly.

"Yes," I say, my voice shaking.

"Well then, it's going to a good cause. But I will be taking my date, just so you know."

A smile spreads across my face. "I can live with that."

He pauses and looks at me earnestly.

"Will you forgive me?"

I feel myself well up with emotion again, and when my voice comes out it's thick with it.

"Yes," I say. "Will you forgive me?"

"There's nothing to forgive," Jonah says. "Franchesca?"

"Yes?"

"I'm going to kiss you now."

"Okay."

He takes a step forward and pulls me into his arms, one hand on the back of my head. My heart is thrumming in my chest, and every inch of my skin is on fire. He feels exactly how I remember, and I melt into him. I have missed this feeling. I have *mourned* this feeling. And now here I am, pressed against him, feeling the steady rhythm of his heart under my hand.

When he presses his lips to mine and kisses me, I feel like I'm home.

Chapter 21

"I still can't believe you bought the dress!" says Robbie, shaking her head in disbelief.

Jonah and I are at Matt and Robbie's house for dinner. Jonah has been staying in Manhattan since the fundraiser, and even though it's only been a week I can barely remember what my apartment looks like. We didn't tell them that we'd been spending time together again until tonight—mainly because we've spent most of it in bed when I'm not at work. Which has also been going way better recently; Jessica has been *much* nicer to me since I inadvertently caused her to run the most financially successful fundraiser the company's ever seen.

"And held onto it for months!" I say.

"What can I say," says Jonah, shrugging. "I'm a man of many talents."

"Oh yeah," says Matt, sarcastically. "I'd need almost one full hand to count them all."

Jonah shoots him a look, and Robbie and I chuckle.

"Sooo," says Robbie, with all the subtlety of a sledgehammer. "I guess that means you two are... an item? Officially?"

"I guess we are," says Jonah, smiling at me. He gives my hand a squeeze under the table.

That's one of the things we've been talking about this past week. Jonah is planning to move to New York. He says it'll be more convenient for visiting Matt anyway, and he seems pretty certain that Matt will agree to move HQ here and leave a satellite office in Chicago for their staff.

When we're done with dinner, Jonah asks Matt if he can have a word in private—I assume to run the plan by him. They head into the study, leaving Robbie and me alone.

"How's your dad?" she asks.

"He's doing great," I say, hardly able to believe it myself. "He got his second chip from AA, he's growing vegetables, he's taking photographs of everything and sending them to me. He calls me every few days to tell me about his tomatoes. He's even started putting on a little weight."

"Wow," says Robbie, her eyes wide. "I'm so happy for you both, Fran. Maybe you could bring him next time you and Jonah come over? We'll serve grape juice instead of wine, of course."

She's been drinking grape juice all night anyway. I'm sure I can do the same in solidarity with my dad.

"He'd love that," I say. "Jonah and I are going to visit him tomorrow, I'll ask him then."

She smiles again, then leans into me conspiratorially. "I always knew you two would end up together," she says, looking very smug.

"You didn't even know you'd end up with Matt until he literally laid siege to your house," I scoff. "When did you get so perceptive?"

"Oh, I don't know," says Robbie. "Maybe it's the hormones."

"I see," I say, nodding. "Wait, what?"

She grins broadly at me.

"Oh my God!" I gasp, shooting to my feet as it hits me. "I'm such an idiot! You'd *never* drink grape juice instead of wine unless…"

"It's really early," she says. "So we're not telling anyone else yet. But I couldn't keep it from you."

"Oh my God!" I shout again, running around the table to grab her into a bear hug. She laughs and hugs me back, giving me a tight squeeze.

"I'm so happy for you!" I tell her, but the words don't begin to convey the feeling. "I knew you had nothing to worry about!"

"We're very happy," she says. "Although Matt is already being overprotective, so I might have to sass his ass back in line soon."

"Are you telling Jonah?" I ask. "Just… so I know."

I'm not sure how I'll manage to keep it from him, given that we're spending every non-working minute together these days.

"Yes," she says. "Matt is probably telling him right now. He was going to ask if Jonah would mind moving their HQ to New York so he won't have to travel so far so often."

I let out a delighted peal of laughter that takes Robbie by surprise.

"What?" she asks, a quizzical look on her face.

"Jonah asked Matt to talk because he wants to move their HQ to Manhattan," I tell her. "And he's moving here himself!"

"Oh!" says Robbie, looking delighted. "Well, isn't that just perfect?"

"Perfect," I say, nodding in agreement.

∼

The guest room in Robbie and Matt's place is beautifully decorated, with a four-poster bed that Jonah and I have just finished making great use of. As we lay there together, with shafts of moonlight slicing between the drapes, Jonah sighs and pulls me close. I curl myself against him, breathless, and run my fingers through the short hairs on his chest, while he traces his fingers up and down my hip.

"So, I was thinking," he says.

"That never ends well," I shoot back.

He pats my ass to chastise me, but it only makes me giggle.

"I'm definitely not suggesting you should give up your apartment," he says. "I know your independence means a lot to you, and you should have a place that's yours."

I always find it interesting when he tells me things about myself that I never even knew he'd picked up on.

"But I'm going to give you a key to my apartment, and you can stay over as often as you like, and leave as much stuff as you want, and if that means all the time and all your stuff, then that'll be just fine by me."

"Are you asking me to move in with you?" I ask, pushing myself up a little so I can look down at his face.

"I'm trying to ask you to move in with me in a way that doesn't make you feel like you wouldn't have any control," he says. "How am I doing?"

I chuckle at him and lean down to steal a kiss from his mouth.

"Pretty good," I say. "But I'll only consider it if you also promise not to get mad when your lovely minimalist apartment ends up strewn with clothes and books."

He feigns a pained expression, and I slap him playfully on the shoulder.

"Fine," he grins, "Your terms are acceptable."

"Okay," I say. "I'll consider it, then."

He lifts an eyebrow at me.

"Okay, I considered it—yes," I blurt, and he laughs and pulls me into a deep kiss.

"I love you, Franchesca Jane Potts," he tells me. "Always have."

"I love you, too, Jonah Wells," I say, grinning. "But it took a little while."

Epilogue

I jump off the yacht, run along the short pier, and sprint along the beach toward Jonah. He's grinning long before I reach him, and he holds his arms out wide for me to jump into. I wrap my arms around his neck, my legs around his waist, and kiss him deeply.

"I missed you," I say when I pull back.

I haven't seen him in five days. He's been away on a series of business meetings, and then he flew straight here in his seaplane while the rest of us took the yacht.

It's all the same faces as last year—plus one. Robbie and Matt's daughter, Elodie, is just the cutest little thing you've ever seen. And she's still so tiny I can barely feel the weight of her when I hold her. She has a new baby smell that is frankly dangerous for a woman in her mid-twenties trying to build a career, and she's too young to do anything but be passed around like a happy little gurgling adorable bundle for everyone to coo over.

"I missed you more," Jonah says with a wide, gorgeous grin on his face. "How was your voyage?"

"Perfect," I say, setting my feet back on the sand as Jonah puts me down. "I got to hold Elodie loads. She's so stinkin' cute."

"She is," he agrees. We *may* be a little biased, considering we're going to be her godparents.

Jonah takes me by the hand, and we stroll back along the beach.

"God, it's so weird being back here," I say. "I can't believe it's been a year."

"Time flies when you're having fun," says Jonah.

"Let's hope there are no storms this time."

"Oh, I don't know," he says. "After five days apart, I could do with being stranded on a desert island with you for a while."

"Smooth-talker," I say, sticking out my tongue at him. "You don't have to drag me to a storm bunker to have your way with me these days."

"I mean, I don't *have* to, but…" he replies, grinning wickedly at me.

A tingle of pleasure rolls up my spine, and I lace my fingers through his.

"Still," I say, thoughtfully, "I suppose if it wasn't for that storm, none of the rest of this would've happened."

"So you'd do it all again?" he asks.

"In a heartbeat," I reply, happily.

"Even hell year?"

"No!" I exclaim, shaking my head furiously. "No, not that. Never again. Give me a hurricane over that, any day."

There's no party this year. Elodie is a little too young, and Robbie is still breastfeeding, so it's just our little group of family and friends. We're going to have a very sensible and grown-up dinner tonight to celebrate Matt and Robbie's second anniversary.

~

"How does this look?" I ask Jonah, turning from the mirror to face him.

I've opted for a pale-yellow maxi dress, sleeveless, and a white shawl with small daisies embroidered into it. My wardrobe is in much better shape these days—partly because I'm being paid better since I graduated hell year and became a fully-fledged accounting intern, and partly because Jonah has somehow managed to trick me into being less weird about him buying things for me.

"Honestly?" he asks.

He does this every time. I roll my eyes in exasperation, but I'm smiling.

"You look better without it."

"You're such a perv," I say, turning away from him to put my earrings in.

"I never used to be," says Jonah. "You're a bad influence. A minx. A wanton seductress who's turned me into a desperate shell of a man, craving your body every moment of the da—"

He cuts off and laughs as I launch a throw cushion at him.

"You look beautiful," he says.

"Thank you."

It's nice to see him relaxed and happy. He's seemed a little on-edge every now and then since I arrived, and I've occasionally found him huddled together with Matt, talking quietly and then breaking apart when I get within earshot. It seems like maybe their latest business deal isn't going too well. I hope he can at least enjoy himself while he's here.

"Shall we go out, then?" I ask.

"Sure."

Jonah gets to his feet and pulls the door open for me. As I walk past, he wolf whistles at me and bites his fist like a cartoon horndog. I giggle and shake my ass at him.

~

Everyone is already at the table when we arrive—well, almost everyone. Elodie is down for a nap, and Trish and Will's boys are engaged in the far more important business of building sandcastles on the beach.

We all chat our way through dinner, although there's not as much to catch up on as last year, now that Jonah is based in Manhattan and we go back to Meadow Hill every other weekend to visit everyone. Jonah has become quite emotionally invested in my dad's pumpkin patch, at this point. He's even talking about entering "the big one" in the town's Harvest Festival.

"Ladies and Gentlemen," says Matt, rising from his seat and chinking his fork against the side of his glass. "If I could have your attention, please."

We all fall silent, and Matt places a hand on Robbie's shoulder. He gives a lovely speech about meeting her and loving her, and gushes without reservation about Elodie and what an amazing mother Robbie is. I notice Jonah is

265

shifting in his seat beside me, patting his pocket, pulling his shirt away from his chest, and clearing his throat.

"But before I ask you all to join me in a toast," Matt says as he rounds out his speech, "I believe there's someone else here who has an announcement to make. Jonah?"

I turn to Jonah in surprise as he stands up from his seat. I didn't know he was planning a speech this year.

"Thanks, Matt," he says. He looks nervous, which is unusual for him. I tilt my head a little as I try to figure out why.

"As you all know, I gave a speech at the party last year."

"A great speech, dear," Brenda chimes in.

"Thanks, Mrs. Wilson," says Jonah with a smile. "It was a speech about love. About finding someone to be with every day. Someone you never get bored of. Someone you can share your pain and your joy with, who will love you through your worst moments and celebrate your best."

Now that I hear these echoes of the speech he gave last year, I remember just how lovely it was.

"And at the time, it was a speech about Robbie and Matt," says Jonah, "who I think we can all agree are just an absolutely perfect match."

"Hear, hear," says Will.

"But it was also about me," he says. "Because I already knew that I'd found the woman I was describing that day."

He reaches his hand into his pocket.

"I already knew the woman who I wanted to be with every day, who I could never get enough of, whose worst moments are better than my best, and whose best moments take my breath away."

He pulls a small box out of his pocket and gets down on one knee beside me, and it's only at that very second I actually realize what's happening.

"Oh!" I cry in surprise and everyone else at the table chuckles. I can feel tears springing suddenly to my eyes. I had no idea. Not a single clue.

"Franchesca Jane Potts," says Jonah, looking up at me with my hand in his. "You are the most amazing woman I've ever met. You're funny and sweet, generous and kind, determined and smart. And you've kicked the ass of every obstacle life's ever thrown at you. I admire you more than anyone, I love you so much it drives me crazy, and I'd be the happiest man in the world if you'd agree to be my someone, forever. Will you marry me?"

I can feel hot tears rolling down my cheeks. The little box in his hand has the most beautiful ring in it, small diamonds set around a larger, emerald-cut diamond in the middle, glittering as his hand shakes slightly in the evening sun.

"Yes!" I say, almost yelling it. "Yes! Are you crazy? Yes, I will marry you!"

He pushes the ring onto my finger and pulls me to my feet, taking me into his strong arms and holding me while everyone around us erupts in applause and cheers.

He leans in and presses a kiss to my lips, then smiles down at me, looking happier than I've ever seen him before.

"I told you she'd say yes!" calls Robbie.

"You knew?" I say, looking scandalized.

"He even asked your dad for permission," grins Matt.

"You did?" I ask Jonah, looking up at him.

"Sure I did," he says. "He told me to take a hike because you make your own decisions."

I laugh, and as another stream of happy tears flows freely down my cheeks, I lean up to kiss my future husband.

Want More?

Can't get enough of Fran and Jonah?

Head to https://geni.us/BonusJonah to read Chapter 10 from Jonah's point of view!

Also by Harmony Knight

Did you miss Robbie and Matt's story? Try
Road Trip with the Billionaire

For some festive frolics in Upstate NY, pick up
My Small-town CEO Scrooge

And if vacation flings and gigantic surprises are your bag,
snuggle up with
Surprise Baby for Christmas

About the Author

Harmony Knight loves reading great romance books, drinking tea, and writing bios in third person.

She was born and raised in an ex-mining village in South Wales (UK), but after kissing her fair share of frogs she found her prince and moved across the Irish Sea. She now lives in Ireland with her family.

Harmony writes the books she loves to read, full of loveable heroines and the caring alpha men who have to have them, and she hopes you'll love to read them, too!

For news and updates, check out her website at www.harmonyknight.com where you can sign up for her mailing list so you'll never miss a release!

Made in the USA
Coppell, TX
16 September 2022